Alex stepped back, then took Lina by the shoulders and turned her around. "I'm user friendly." She smiled just slightly, then took Lina's hands and held them against her cheeks. "Monitor..." She pulled them gently down her neck, around the curve of her breasts, across her belly. "Keyboard..." She tucked them between her legs, gathering her dress between her thighs. "Mouse..." She spoke the words right into Lina's mouth, as their lips brushed together. "How scary is this?" she whispered.

Lina wasn't sure if she said "terrifying" or just thought it.

About the Author

Mindy Kaplan was born in Philadelphia, reared in Miami and is currently growing up in Vancouver. In this lifetime she has incarnated as a psychologist, a university professor, a writer of novels and screenplays, a film director, and the doting mother to six cats (so far). Her feature film, *Devotion,* is now available on video and has also been published as a Naiad novel.

THE GIRL
NEXT DOOR
BY MINDY KAPLAN

THE NAIAD PRESS, INC.
1996

Printed in the United States of America on acid-free paper
First Edition

Editor: Karin Kallmaker
Cover designer: Bonnie Liss (Phoenix Graphics)
Typesetter: Sandi Stancil

Library of Congress Cataloging-in-Publication Data

Kaplan, Mindy, 1961 –
    The girl next door / by Mindy Kaplan.
        p.   cm.
    ISBN 1-56280-140-6
    I. Title.
PS3561.A5637G57   1996
813'.54—dc20

96-8545
CIP

*This book is dedicated to my grandmother,
who told me it should have "more sex" in it
than my last book (and so it does) —
to my mother, whom I love and respect more
with each passing year and am proud
to call a friend —
and to Cathy Robertson, who continues
to open my heart and my eyes
in the most fantastic ways.*

And to Heba, who will always be my Prince.

1

AN OBSIDIAN TOWER STRETCHES TOWARD AN ICY
CRESCENT MOON. CRUMBLING, IT PLAYS TRICKS
ON THE EYE, LOOKING MUCH LIKE A DARK
ANGEL AS IT FADES AND DISAPPEARS. THUNDER
YAPS AT ITS HEELS, AND EVEN THE MOST
INTENSE BOLTS OF BLUE-WHITE CANNOT
ILLUMINATE THREE HUNDRED AND SIXTY
DEGREES OF DARKNESS.

The lime-green cursor spiraled across the glowing
screen, and Lina could feel the slide of sweat beneath

her fingertips. She locked her hands together to stop their shaking, then firmly gripped the mouse. Using both hands, she zeroed in on the SAVE icon and double-clicked. There was no more to be written. The images were gone.

She unlatched the bedroom window and leaned out into the night. The sky was pitch black and patched with stars that twinkled leisurely. Although the rain had stopped, each kick of the wind sent droplets spraying down from the fir trees to tap against the patio. Judging by the moon's position, there was still plenty of time to sleep before morning.

She untangled her damp sheets and remade the bed. So what if the dreams were back? She'd cope with them like the nuisance they were. She fluffed her pillow and checked the room — she wasn't sure for what — but satisfied with the look of things, she slid back into bed. The thermostat was set at a cool seventy-two degrees and the rain was beginning again.

"How come these boxes are here?" Sean's voice yanked Lina into the new day. "The big hand is on the six and the little hand is on the seven!" He tugged on her nightshirt.

Lina opened one eye and glanced sideways at him. It couldn't possibly be time to wake up — she'd just fallen back to sleep. But sure enough, yellow sunlight was spilling in through the east window, seemingly intent on blinding her.

"Up." She patted the bed and cursed herself for not rehanging the curtain rod. Apparently it was never meant to hold wet clothes. Sean swung a leg up and she pulled him the rest of the way. "And?" She raised her brow. Sean leaned and kissed her sweetly on the cheek.

"How come your stuff's like that?" He pointed to the row of cartons lined against the far wall.

"You know why, honey." She wiped dried toothpaste from the corner of his mouth. "We talked about it. Remember?" Before Sean could answer, an ear-piercing screech came from outside. *"Merde . . ."* Lina jumped up and got to the window just in time to see a green Miata plant itself in the artemisia bed, several feet short of the pool.

"Darling . . . ?" Claire Elliason was already on her way to the door. Lina could hear her heels clicking swiftly down the hall and out onto the tiled veranda. "Is that you?"

Sean dashed outside behind his mother, but Lina stayed put. Framed by the window, she saw a pair of tanned legs swing over the car door and slide down into the mangled vegetation. Alexandra Wilder stumbled forward a few steps and raised an invisible glass in toast. "Hello, Mother."

Claire shook her head in exasperation. "It seems we'll have to replant." They hugged politely.

Lina shifted to avoid being seen. Alex looked different than she did in the living room portrait. She appeared more angular, unpolished, almost roguish. Her denim shorts were frayed up to her underwear, and her long legs tucked down into mud-coated hiking boots. The wind had whipped her auburn waves into a tangle and mirrored Ray-Bans hid her green eyes. But this state of dishevelment only magnified her good looks and Alex obviously

3

knew it. What Lina knew was trouble when she saw it.

"Hey little boy." Alex nodded at Sean and dug something from her pocket. He reached for it immediately and took off toward the car. "Good pool day." She lifted her shirt, exposing her belly. "Amazing sun!" She trudged toward the house. "Gotta love it!"

Claire pulled her heels from the soil and veered onto the driveway, clicking closely behind.

"*Mon Dieu . . .*" Lina grabbed her outfit from the doorknob and dressed quickly. On her way down the hall, she framed herself in the Louis the Fourteenth mirror and tried on several expressions. None of them made her look any less tired. Her dark eyes were still puffed with slumber, her full lips slightly downturned from their press against the pillow. She licked several fingers and smoothed her black hair, curling it under slightly at the shoulder. She reached up beneath her skirt and pulled her blouse down flat.

"I've been on the road for ten days and eaten nothing but Subways and Butterfingers," Alex's voice trailed down the hall and Lina ducked into the butler's pantry. Backed against a shelf full of family-sized cereal boxes and canned goods, Lina pulled her skirt back down into place. She heard the clank of jars and bottles as Alex yanked the refrigerator open. "Got any hollandaise sauce?"

"Hollandaise sauce isn't something you *have* dear . . ." Claire tittered. "It's something you *make*."

Lina tilted her head and peeked through the wooden slats of the pantry door. Alex had her head in the refrigerator, and Claire was eyeing her own reflection in the stainless steel door. "Jean Pierre

4

thinks I should go brunette again." She poked at her hair with several fingers. "He had the color mixed before I even arrived. I told him, 'I pay the bill, I pick the color.' Can you imagine?" She pulled a lipstick from under her bra strap and gave her lips a quick Fiery Cinnamon touch-up. "Want some, darling? It would be so pretty with your eyes."

"Yeah, right." Alex pulled out a bottle of Snapple and kicked the door closed.

Claire stuck the lipstick back under her shirt. "You know, we expected you home days ago."

"I met these guys in Montana." Alex twisted off the lid and gulped her tea. "They were camping and I was exhausted. So I stayed awhile."

"Montana? How silly, dear. What could there possibly be in Montana for a young woman from Haddon Park?"

"The water was terrific. Cold as shit, though."

"Oh dear. Why didn't you stop somewhere civilized, like New York?"

"I left from Jersey, Mom."

"It just doesn't make sense to me."

"It doesn't need to. Got any tuna?"

"I thought you were a vegetabalist."

"Vegetarian, Mother. No meat."

"But fish . . ."

"Tuna. Tuna is not fish. It comes in a can, for Christsake."

Claire wrung her hands. "It's probably somewhere. Maybe up there." She gestured randomly to a row of cabinets.

Lina craned around the pantry door and peeked into the kitchen. "Tuna isn't fish?" she mumbled under her breath.

5

"Hey. What are you doing in there?" Lina turned and spotted Sean halfway down the hall, tugging a black duffel bag behind him. She put her fingers to her lips.

"Hey!" Alex came around the corner. "My car keys?" She extended a hand to Sean, who turned them over with a proud grin. "Bag over there." She pointed toward her room.

"I'll transfer it." Lina quickly lifted the bag and swung it over her shoulder. Alex's eyes locked on her.

"Who're you?"

"This is Lina, dear. Lina Marsalis." Claire hurried out to join them. "I told you about her. Remember?"

Alex pulled a pack of Camels from her shorts. "The baby-sitter." Lina cringed.

"Au pair, darling," Claire corrected.

"Whatever." Alex strolled to the stove and dangled her cigarette into the flame.

"Not in here, Alexandra. You know better."

She took a single puff, then mashed the rest on the sole of her boot and stuffed it down the garbage disposal.

"Your father will be home at six fifteen. He's bringing take-out from La Cocina."

"He's not my father." Alex flipped on the garbage disposal.

"We'll eat at six thirty." Claire turned to Lina. "You're welcome to join us, of course."

Lina was horrified by the thought. "Of course. Thank you." She nodded. "Six thirty, then."

* * * * *

6

Sean helped Lina tug the last carton across the pebbled patio. He stopped and looked up at her as they rounded the diving board. "Why're you sleeping in the pool house?"

"The *guest* house ..." Lina caught herself parroting Claire's euphemism. She'd learn to talk the talk of Haddon Park. She wasn't proud of it, but propriety was a hard thing to shake, and second nature to a diplomat's daughter. She knelt beside Sean. "Remember when we went on the boat ride in Green Lake Park?"

He scrunched his face in thought. "We paddled with our feet," he recalled proudly.

"Right. And what did we talk about?"

He pushed a thumb under his Indian bead belt. "We got *this* from the man with the hair like a girl's."

"Yes, we did." Lina put her hands around his waist. "Sean, where have I been sleeping?" He shrugged, and she waited.

"Alex's room," he mumbled reluctantly.

"And?"

"You could stay in my room."

"That's sweet, but I want to stay out here in the ... pool house."

"You could stay in Grandma's old room. She lives at the gray yard now."

"Grave yard ... honey." She fumbled for words, muted by his candor. "Listen to me. I'll be right here next door and you can come visit me anytime you want. OK?"

He nodded reluctantly. Lina knew he didn't understand, but she couldn't explain it any further.

7

She liked her routine, and she realized that her presence somehow completed the Elliason family. But, come summer's end, she'd be on her way back home. Best to start separating now and ease the blow. And Alex's arrival provided the perfect vehicle for her own departure.

She put Sean to work unpacking her shirts and stacking them into piles according to color. He'd been learning to categorize at the Whiz Kidz program, and putting his free time to "good use" was a part of Lina's mandate. But she took wide latitude in defining what "good use" meant, and typically used his interest level as a barometer. So far, it was working well for both of them.

She hadn't always been sure it would. She almost hadn't accepted the position when Nathan Elliason first offered it to her last September. But she'd been one-week-new to Seattle, and the offer included escape from dorm life, which she already detested. Besides, Nathan's plea had been compelling. She remembered him telling his secretary to hold all calls, then pacing behind his huge leather chair, hands shoved deep in his pockets.

"In my twelve years at this University, you are the first student to come into this office of your own volition," he'd declared. "Serious and ambitious. I respect that."

She'd struggled to graciously receive his praise, but the truth was that she was simply following through on her father's counsel. "Let the decision makers see your face," he'd told her as they'd hugged good-bye at the airport. But that was a point she needn't share with the provost, who was aiming a serious look her way.

"I have a four-year-old son," Nathan explained. "My wife and I are very busy people, you understand. I work some seventy hours a week between here and my remaining law practice. And Claire, that's my wife, she has . . . well, you understand, obligations and such."

The pains he'd taken to choose his words piqued her curiosity. She'd since come to understand that Claire's "obligations" amounted to shopping and lunching with the wives of other administrators, attending fund raisers and cocktail parties, and the occasional "R and R" check-in at the local health spa slash psych unit. But at the time, it was clear only that Nathan's concern about his son was genuine, and that pushed all the right buttons for Lina.

"We want Sean, that's our boy, to have the best of care. And your matriculation papers indicate that you've had a year of graduate study in Childhood Psychology." He motioned to a folder on his desk. "I hope you don't mind, I did a little checking. We've been looking for someone for almost a year, and I just thought perhaps . . ." He rolled his chair back and sat down, crossing his hands on the desk in front of him. "Claire will need to interview you, if you're interested, that is. And if she approves, we'll provide you with a stipend. And, of course, room and board."

As it turned out, the "interview" consisted of being sat down by Claire to watch an episode of Sally Jessy Raphael. The topic was "High Maintenance

9

Children", and Claire had suspected that Sean might "be like that." She wanted Lina to watch the show, then give her opinion and recommendation. Lina agreed to the assignment and the job.

What she'd since discovered was that Sean had an abundance of energy and a keen attunement to everything going on around him. He also had an uncanny knack for asking questions that somehow pointed her directly to things she needed to be thinking about. And if he liked to be pushed endlessly on the swinging tire or engaged in a game of tackle football while sharing his mind, it seemed a small price to pay. She'd reported this verdict back to a relieved Claire, who subsequently reversed her decision to sign Sean up at her spa for "behavior management" and checked herself in instead.

Lina watched Sean now across the room, finger to his lips, trying to determine whether to put her rust colored sweater in the red pile or the brown one. The workings of his mind tick-tocked across his plump face, and she resisted the urge to suggest a solution. After a moment, he cleared a space and created a new pile. Why hadn't that occurred to her?

She looked around her new room, a place she'd been in many times before but never really seen. A four-poster bed, used routinely by intoxicated party-goers who stumbled west of poolside in unsanctified pairs. An ornate dresser with matching stool and hanging mirror, not Louis the Fourteenth but a good imitation. Six candleless sconces collected from ports around the world. An antique standing phone with an ivory handle beside a carved desk covered by too many layers of paint. A view out the bay windows of the gardens, the main quarters, the pool. A com-

fortable space, and blessedly away from the house . . .
which, she reminded herself, was why she was there.

She flipped back the flaps of the last carton and
dug through its contents: her laptop computer and
school books, a tattered Amelia Earhart birthday
card, the cork from a bottle of cabernet she'd shared
with her father the night before leaving Athens. For
the first time since she'd left, she felt a pang of
homesickness. She pulled her laptop and several
books from the carton, then pushed it into the closet.
All she really needed were her clothes. She'd be gone
after summer semester anyway.

She put Sean down for a nap and hummed to
him until he fell asleep, then unplugged the phone
and retrieved her laptop. She plugged her modem
into the phone jack, and stretched the cord across the
room so she could curl into the recessed seating by
the bay window. She and her father had agreed to
communicate regularly via electronic mail, as it was
less expensive and, more to the point, he was
virtually impossible to reach by phone. She'd been
more diligent than he, composing weekly assurances
that it had been a good decision for her to spend this
year in the States, and that she would indeed be
returning to Athens as planned. It was a source of
contention, given her mother's legacy, but she'd been
meticulous in preparing her case and ultimately had
simply out-negotiated him. She flipped open her
laptop and dialed into the World CompuLine. A
palette of colorful icons spread their welcome across
the screen, offering the thrill of anonymous social
mix and match. Click here to shop. Click here to
complain. Click here to meet the love of your life.
She'd done some exploring the first few times she'd

signed on, but had since disciplined herself to access the internet directly and pull up her father's e-mail address — and when the familiar cursor finally signaled, she began typing as always:

MON CHER PERE, TOUT VA BIEN ICI...

2

"Your hair looks better down, Mom," Alex opined through a mouthful of burrito.

Lina caught Claire's injured look from across the dining room table. Just the slightest flash of disappointment in her eyes, a twitching of her lipsticked mouth.

"Be a darling and pass the chips, would you?" Claire turned her attention to Lina.

"I think the barrette looks nice," Lina offered with the nachos.

"Lovely dear," Nathan confirmed. "Mother of pearl, isn't it?" Claire nodded.

Sean looked at Alex, confused. "You gave her that."

"Well that was then, little boy." Alex gulped her Snapple. "And this is now."

Alex's tone irked Lina, and she regretted having given up her usual chair so that Sean could sit by Alex.

Claire leaned and touched Lina's arm. "Alex always was fickle like that," she explained. "When she was little, just about Sean's age I think, she begged and begged Richard, that's her father, to get her a bicycle. Her little friend just across the street had one . . . what was her name, darling?"

"Sheri." Alex burped just loud enough to be heard, which Lina found crass and Sean found hysterical.

"Of course." Claire didn't miss a beat. "Sheri had one. A lovely little bike with streamers and one of those cute little horns that tooted when you squeezed them. Toot-toot, toot-toot." She laughed. Lina refused to look Alex's way, anticipating her derisive look. "We didn't have a lot of money back then, but Richard always was a pushover when it came to this one." Claire nodded in Alex's direction. "And so you won't be surprised when I tell you he finally went out and bought her a bicycle just like Sheri's. Well, the scene Alex made when he gave it to her was simply frightful."

"It was embarrassing, Mom," Alex defended. "Who

wants the exact same bike as someone right across the street?"

"Mine's just like Mark's," Sean offered. "I like it. We're twins!"

"Well," Claire continued, "Alex picked that bike right up, little thing that she was, and threw it right off the front porch. Her father didn't know whether to laugh or throttle her."

"And I had to ride that banged up piece of crap for two years after that," Alex grumbled. Claire dabbed her lips with her napkin, and Lina was sure she was hiding a smile.

"Mine has a racing stripe and Mark's doesn't," Sean persisted, "So I think we're not really twins. We're not really twins, Alex." He checked for approval, which was not forthcoming.

"Your bike is lovely," Lina offered.

"And you're a fine rider, son," Nathan assured.

"Quite, darling," Claire confirmed, then turned to Alex with a smile. "Your father and I have a surprise for you."

"He's not my father."

Nathan didn't flinch. Lina checked.

"What's the surprise?" Sean scanned the dining room.

"It's in the foyer son," Nathan replied. "On the table. You can get it and bring it in if you'd like."

Sean was gone before Nathan finished his sentence, and quickly returned with the wrapped package. "I got it." He handed it to Alex. "Here's our surprise."

"*Our* surprise, huh?" Alex took the box from his hands. "Well, let's see what our surprise is."

Everyone waited silently as Alex ripped through the paper and slid the thin computer from its wrapping. Her expression was noncommittal.

"We thought it might help you to have this, in case you have any work to do." Claire explained hopefully.

"We know you have work to do." Nathan took a stronger stance. "A term paper still outstanding from your archeology class, I believe?"

"Where's the paperwork?" Alex pushed her plate aside and laid the computer on the table. "The warranty and stuff?"

"I upgraded to a Pentium last month. An administrative perk." Nathan smiled at Lina, as though there were some bond they shared by virtue of their affiliation with the university. Lina caught where Nathan was leading, and resisted inclusion.

Alex caught the gist too. "So this is a hand-me-down," she scoffed.

"Lina has one just like it," Claire offered, trying to save the day in her oblivious way.

Visions of bicycles flashed through Lina's mind as she waited for the proverbial shit to hit the fan.

"Is that so?" Alex fixed her stare on Lina.

"Well, yes..." Lina squirmed. "I mean, mine's not exactly the same..."

"It's close enough, darling," Claire interrupted. "Isn't it?"

Close enough for what, Lina wondered. "Yes, it's close enough, I suppose." She looked at Alex. "But not really the same, you know. I'm sure yours has... more RAM."

Nathan clarified. "We were hoping that Lina would be willing to work with you, Alex. To show you the ropes, shall we say, of using the computer."

Lina wished she could sink into the floor.

"She's been so good with Sean, darling. Taught him so many things. And we just thought maybe she could help you too, with your . . . ," Claire motioned to the computer, "lap thing."

"I go to college, Mother!" Alex glared at Claire. "I know how to use a computer!"

Lina was as anxious to be paired with Alex as an ox is to be yoked to a kangaroo. She decided this would be a good time to clear the table. "Excuse me." She collected the plates quickly and disappeared into the kitchen. She could feel Alex's eyes on her back as she left the room.

Lina slipped into a nightshirt and prepared for bed, relieved that the day had finally come to an end. On her way out of the house, Claire and Nathan had cornered her in the foyer and pleaded their case that she spend some time with Alex and "get her on the right track." Sensing that their agenda extended beyond mere computer tutoring, Lina had backed quickly into the drizzly night, with only an uneasy promise to try her best.

She switched off the light and lay stiff in her new bed. The pillows were too stuffed, the mattress too hard, the posts looked like strange creatures reaching toward the ceiling. The pool lights shone through the bay window, casting shifting patterns of light and shadow across the walls. She'd always liked that back in her other room — Alex's room. The water would reflect tiny diamonds against the ceiling, and she'd pretend they were stars and stare at them until she became mesmerized and fell asleep. But in this room there were no stars, only long, dark fingers of shadow that stretched around her, daring her to fall asleep in their grip.

She pulled the sheets back and swung her feet over the side of the bed and straight into her moccasins. Still her favorite shoes, they'd been relegated to bedwear status years ago, when she'd made the minor faux pas of wearing them to a party at the French embassy in Greece. Most of the dignitaries had seemed amused, but her father clearly was not. He'd escorted her to the door and sent her home with the driver, extracting a promise that she'd throw them away before he arrived home. She did, in her bedroom wastebasket, but only until the next morning when she brokered their retrieval over breakfast. She'd found it easy to beat her father at his own game, but the skill was itself a guilty pleasure that she only brought to bear on matters of the heart . . . like moccasins and trips to the States.

She unhooked the curtains and began to draw them closed. The cobalt-tiled pool glistened in the night, and a slight steam rose from the water. Alex was still awake. Her lights were on, though Lina didn't see her anywhere in the room. She pulled the curtains closed and checked the room for long, dark fingers. They were gone. She laid back in bed and stared at the ceiling until she fell asleep.

18

3

Sean was already up and brushing his teeth when Lina came in. "Look!" He curled his lips back to show his work.

"Hmm." Lina inspected them playfully. "Good job. But I think I see some bird feathers back there. Have you been prowling around again at night?"

Sean giggled. "Uh-uh."

"Well, if you don't finish your breakfast we'll know for sure."

"Peanut butter!" He jumped into the air.

"You can have peanut butter on your toast, *with*

your cereal." Lina nudged him out of the bathroom. "Now, pick out your clothes."

Sean slid open his closet and pointed up at a polo shirt. "It's blue day."

"Yes." Lina looked down at her own blouse. "It's blue day." Sean almost always wore the same color clothes as her. He thought it somehow made him her brother, although they'd had the talk about Lina not having any siblings. She'd actually grown to like it, but knew she had to phase it out as part of her disengagement. "How about this one?" She pulled out his favorite football jersey and handed it to him. He looked up at her, confused.

"Not purple." He shook his head. "That one." He pointed again to the blue polo. She rehung the jersey and gave him the shirt he wanted, saving the battle for some other day.

Alex was notably absent during the morning flurry of activity, though Lina heard Claire knocking on her door repeatedly, announcing whatever was going on in the house. "We're just about to serve breakfast, darling. As soon as the bacon's done." And then it was "Breakfast is almost over, dear. There's still some toast, but it's cold." Followed by "Your grandmother's on the phone. Line two. Be a good girl and say hello."

But only silence and an occasional grunt came back through the door. Alex wasn't biting. Lina would have broken hours ago. She couldn't bear the sight of Claire pacing around the house with that fretting look, just searching for the next excuse to bang on Alex's door. Certainly when Alex finally emerged she would be steeped in guilt.

But when Alex did get up, time unknown, she'd simply slinked unnoticed out to the pool. Lina caught sight of her from the den, where she was engaged in a serious Nintendo battle with Sean. From her position, she could see only Alex's long legs and a triangular swatch of ruby red bikini. She stretched for a better look.

"Gotcha." Sean blasted her fighter jet into tiny silver pieces.

"Time out." Lina stood and casually moved to the French doors for a better look. Alex was draped, coma like, over a lounge chair — headphones on, laptop precariously balanced on her oiled belly. "She shouldn't have her computer like that." Lina forced her eyes to fix on the machine.

"Huh?" Sean came to Lina's side and looked where he saw her looking. In a flash, he was out the door.

"*Mon Dieu* . . ." Lina took off behind him.

"Heyyyy!" Sean screeched on his way across the patio.

Lina grabbed him from behind, but not before Alex's green eyes struggled open and locked on them.

"Sorry." Lina forced a smile past Alex's glare.

"You could come play Nintendo!" Sean urged.

Alex pulled her headphones down around her neck. "I'm working." She lowered her Ray-Bans over her eyes, and Lina could see the computer screen reflected in her lenses. Blackjack — and she was doing well.

"Me and Lina could put on our bathing suits and you and me and her could go in the pool," Sean persisted.

"I don't want to go in the pool." Alex pushed herself up with some effort and pulled a pack of cigarettes from her computer case. "I'm busy."

"How much money did you start with?" Lina challenged, annoyed by Alex's callousness.

"Huh?" Alex missed the segue. Lina nodded toward the screen. "Oh that. The usual. A thousand."

She was up to thirty-two thousand now. "High stakes."

"Not really. You just have to take risks." Alex lit her smoke. "Pay to play."

"Well the risk–reward ratio doesn't run in your favor. The odds . . ."

Alex rolled her eyes. "If I lose, I quit the game and start over."

Sean grinned. "That's cheating."

"That's strategy," Alex corrected.

Lina found the defense self-serving, but oddly hard to dispute. "Well, that's not real life."

"What's real life?" Alex pressed her fingers to her temples. "No wait . . ." She feigned concentration. "You work here, you go to school, you come back here to work. Maybe do some homework in between. Probably don't have blackjack on your laptop." She looked up, framing Lina's reflection in her lenses. "How am I doing so far?"

Lina straightened her blouse. "Rather reductionistic."

"Rather ascetic," Alex countered.

"Ascetic?" Big word for Alex. She probably didn't know what it meant.

"Self-denying. Austere." Alex puffed her cigarette, obviously accustomed to being underestimated.

"From the Greek word 'askein'." Lina covered her tracks. "To train the body."

"You know Greek?"

"I live in Greece. I'm French by birth, though."

"Ah, the accent." Alex's expression softened. "I love French. But who doesn't? I mean, especially in bed, you know? Just the sound of it . . ." She laid back and closed her eyes.

Sean perked up. "You mean the people in your dreams talk French?"

Alex cracked a half-smile. "Something like that."

"How do you know what they're saying?" He puckered his face.

"It doesn't matter." She laughed and slid down in her chair.

Lina quickly pulled her gaze from the curve of Alex's belly and crouched in front of Sean. "What do the people in *your* dreams talk about?"

He thought for a moment. "They don't talk about anything. They just do stuff."

"Well, how about if we go do stuff now?"

Sean tugged at Alex's arm. "You could come with us!"

"I already told you I'm busy."

Lina pointed to her watch. "It's almost time for your piano lesson, honey."

"Peanut butter first, please?" Sean made his eyes big, a trick he'd picked up from his mother. It usually worked well for them both.

"Peanut butter with bananas, and a glass of milk."

"Do you want some peanut butter and bananas?" Sean looked at Alex, who only shook her head.

"C'mon then." Lina headed for the house and hoped Sean would follow. "It's you and me."

Sean traipsed reluctantly behind her. "She doesn't like me."

"What, honey?"

"Alex hates me."

Lina pulled open the French doors and steered Sean toward the kitchen. "Why do you think that?"

He turned and stared at her as if the answer were obvious. "Because I came out of Daddy's stomach and she didn't."

It took Lina a second to catch on. "You mean because she has a different father than you?" He nodded. "But you have the same mother, sweetie. She's still your sister."

"One-half sister," he corrected. "And she hates Mommy too."

"I don't think she hates you or your Mom." Lina ushered him into the kitchen and lifted him onto the counter. "She doesn't even know you very well, does she?"

"She stays in her room and I can't get in. Or else she sneaks on Daddy's boat . . ." Sean caught himself and put a hand over his mouth. "I'm not supposed to tell."

"Your secret's safe with me." Lina moved his hand and stuffed a banana slice into his mouth.

"Now let's have some lunch and not worry about Alex, OK?"

Sean squished banana through his teeth and Lina took that as a "yes."

4

THEREFORE, WHEN A PAST TRAUMA PRESENTS
ITSELF IN THE FORM OF A DREAM, IT ACTUALLY
CREATES THE VERY LANGUAGE NECESSARY TO
NAME AND THEREBY DISEMPOWER IT.
ALTHOUGH SUCH DREAM-WORK IS STILL
CONSIDERED LIMITED IN THERAPEUTIC
APPLICATION, IT CAN OPERATE MUCH LIKE THE
TINY HOLE IN THE DIKE THAT ULTIMATELY
FLOODS THE LAND. ONCE A RIGID STRUCTURE
HAS BEEN BROKEN THROUGH IN ANY WAY, THE
CRACK TENDS TO KEEP TRAVELING.

Lina leaned back and stretched her fingers. She'd been typing for . . . how long now? It seemed like the whole evening had gotten away from her. Her term paper was due at noon, and it was already two a.m. It wasn't like her to put off work until the last minute, but she'd managed to avoid this particular assignment for weeks.

It had seemed like the perfect solution at first — she could research the dreams she was having *and* get credit for it at school. But rather than helping to eliminate the nightmares, her research had instead opened the door for them to invade her waking life as well. She'd read all the books and studied the theories, but she would've gladly traded the "A" she was certain to get on the paper for two nights in a row of good sleep.

She rolled her chair back and stretched, bending to push her palms against the floor. Her back seemed to crack in a hundred places, and she felt taller when she stood up. She slid the window open and let in the cool night air. Alex was still awake, propped up on her bed in a white linen robe. Her hair was wet and pulled back in a band. She was talking on the phone, laughing a lot. The boyfriend, Lina figured. But what business was it of hers, and besides, there was work to be done.

She would have gone back to her desk right then, had Alex not reached for a plastic bottle on her night table and begun squeezing lines of baby oil down her outstretched legs. An athlete's legs, Lina mused, with a natural tone that matched the lines of her body and didn't cry "gym." She meant not to watch as Alex worked the oil into her skin, her fingers drawing upward along her calves and thighs, her

27

white robe parting slightly, hands disappearing beneath the linen, rising and falling in a slow, circular motion. She wished she'd never seen any of it, and was relieved to turn away when she finally did.

She felt flushed, and tightly covered her eyes with both hands. This wasn't right. She could be fired in an instant. Maybe even deported. And then her father would be totally disgraced. Her heart pounded, and she tried to pace her breathing. She hated feeling so out of control. This had to be dealt with now.

It began to drizzle just as Lina locked her bike to the stop sign and discreetly slipped out of her biking shorts. She quickly smoothed her skirt and hair, then ducked into the club.

Dark and private, the after-hours hangout was a well kept secret — one of many that she'd managed to uncover all the way from Athens, via modem. Rooting through Seattle's tax data base, which was not public domain and had taken her hours to access, she'd noticed a listing for a business that was jointly owned by two women with the same hyphenated surname. Figuring it might serve as a good place to meet people once she arrived, she quickly downloaded the name and address, then proceeded with her original search.

She'd been to Corridors several times now, but the place still unnerved her a bit. The bodies, wrapped and writhing on the elevated dance floor... purple, green, red lights flashing... music pulsing.

Huge screens hanging from the rafters, running continuous videos of women in various stages of undress and lovemaking. Muffled laughter and the faint smell of hashish drifting from the back deck into the night. And the corridors themselves, where shadowy silhouettes lined concrete walls in silent invitation.

"Buy you a drink?" A deep voice beckoned Lina from behind. She turned, startled by the woman's closeness, then by the blueness of her eyes. The woman smiled and ran a hand through her dark hair. Spinning lights splashed her ivory skin with color. "Drink?"

Lina was tempted. It was hard not to wonder what those eyes would like through the clearness of a vodka on ice. But drinks led to conversation, and she didn't want to get that involved. "No, thank you."

"Then perhaps dance . . . *avec moi*?"

Lina smiled. "My accent?"

"*Oui*." The woman extended a hand. "Nicole."

Lina always hated this part. "Pascal." She reached and took Nicole's hand.

"Pleasure . . ." Nicole lifted Lina's hand to her lips and gently kissed her palm. "To meet you." Lina felt her stomach knot and glanced toward the door. "So . . ." Nicole began to circle around her. "No dance . . ." She slowly moved behind her. "No drink . . ." She ran a hand up the back of Lina's neck and took gentle hold of her hair. "The corridors . . . perhaps?" Lina felt Nicole's breath against her neck and let out a soft moan without meaning to. Nicole slid an arm around her from behind. "That's a yes . . . right?"

Lina hated being forced to say it, but that was part of the game. "Yes," she whispered.

29

"Yes?" Nicole pulled her closer.

"Yes," she said louder, and instantly felt the hot press of Nicole's body against her, guiding her from behind into the web of dark halls. She kept her eyes straight ahead, and tried to ignore the feel of others' eyes on her body as she passed. The music faded behind them until only silence mixed into the darkness. And then she felt the sudden push of Nicole's fingertips against her shoulders, and found herself pinned face forward against the cold wall. A blue lightbulb swung from metal grating overhead, casting a surreal glow down the remaining length of empty hallway. She heard the faint echo of her skirt unzipping and dropping to the floor. And then Nicole's hands were on her bare skin, traveling up the backs of her thighs, sliding beneath her panties, pulling them down into a knot around her ankles. She felt the full weight of Nicole's body press against her, the rough scratch of denim against her exposed skin, the growing wetness of her own want. Her muscles tensed at the feel of Nicole's teeth scraping down her neck and digging into her shoulder. She braced herself against the wall. "Alex . . ."

Nicole stepped back. She took Lina by the shoulders and turned her around. "Right . . ." She lifted Lina's chin to meet her gaze. "I'm Alex . . ." she whispered. Lina's lips trembled slightly, and Nicole pressed two fingers gently against them. "I'm Alex."

Lina pretended that blue eyes were green, as Nicole's free hand reached up and unbuttoned her shirt. She watched as Nicole's lips brushed gently across her breasts, slowly back and forth, taking one nipple then the other between them. And then she

30

leaned her head back and stared up at the dim blue light — releasing her entire body to the singular sensation of the mouth now traveling down her belly, the strong hands parting her thighs, the tongue whirling between her legs. Still bound at the ankles, her knees began to tremble and she cupped her hands around Nicole's head for support. A finger slipped inside her, then another, sending tiny quakes rocking through her body. Head thrown back, she muffled a cry as her body twisted and slid to the ground. Images of oiled hands circling beneath white linen flashed against her closed eyes, and she banished them willfully into the night.

She used the ride home to debrief. The rain had subsided, but puddles splashed up from the ground beneath her tires, spraying a refreshing coolness against her back. The good-byes had been quick. The agreement: not to speak if they ever saw each other again. It was rare that Lina even set out on such missions, and she wasn't proud of them. But Alex had prodded her libido out of dormancy, and surely this . . . release . . . was the lesser of two evils.

Alex's light was still on when Lina pulled her bike up to the cabana. But thankfully her true nemesis, temptation, had abated. Her paper was due in seven hours, and she had precious little time left to sleep before she had to return to writing. But everything was under control now, all would be well.

The morning had been hectic, starting with the discovery of a bite mark on the back of her left shoulder. Sean had to be dropped off at his

Gymboree class, forcing her to be stuck in traffic in Claire's Lexus instead of zooming through the back streets on her bike, and making her late to class for the first time. But the paper got turned in, and she headed home with the big plan of catching a nap before collecting Sean.

As she pulled into the driveway, she could see Alex in her usual spot by the pool, computer on her lap. There was no way to get around her, so Lina checked her hair in the mirror and mustered a confident stride toward the patio. As she got closer, she noticed the phone cord winding from Alex's laptop into the house. Apparently Alex was learning quickly, and without her help.

"Hey," Alex called and waved two fingers in the air. Lina veered toward her, trying to appear casual despite the dress clothes she'd worn to school, despite the sight of Alex's long body stretched in the sun and greased with Bain de Soleil. "Ever heard of a modem?" Alex lifted her sunglasses and squinted up at Lina.

Lina monitored her tone for condescension. "Yes."

"This guy Pete from school, his real name's Gepetto, which is pretty funny cos he's from Tennessee but his mom was really into Disney or something, so we always tease each other about names . . ." Alex stopped short. "Anyway, he spent all last night explaining to me about this thing, the World CompuLine. Sounds ominous, huh? I never tried it before, but he told me about all these 'rooms'. Do you know about rooms?"

Lina knew this was a lose/lose situation. To say she didn't would invite explanation. To say she did would, well, portray her wrongly. And to denounce them would only egg Alex on. That much Lina had picked up already. "I know of them." Truthful, vague and noncommittal.

"Pretty cool, huh?" Alex winked, like an inside joke had passed between them.

Lina didn't want to share the moment. "I use e-mail to communicate with my father."

"In Greece?" Lina nodded. "Damn . . . I've only made it as far as the rooms. And who knows where those people really are? It's probably just, like, ten dorky guys that work for the online company, and they just sit there all day and talk to you so you'll stay online forever and run up your bill."

Lina wondered what possessed Alex to think up something so conspiratorial. She also thought it might be true. "You've watched too many Oliver Stone movies," she quipped. "Either that or too much time in the sun."

Alex's face lit with a smile. "So . . . the woman has a sense of humor." She typed something on her keyboard. "Hang on while I sign offline. No use paying *them* to talk to *you*." She powered down and closed her laptop. "Everybody lies about that stuff anyway."

"What stuff?"

"Oh, everything, really. Who they are, where they are, what they do, who they fuck."

Lina wondered if that remark was intended to shock her. "You've figured all that out already?"

"Uh-uh. Pete-Gepetto told me. But really what he was saying was I should be, you know, careful."

"About?"

"The whole anonymous cyber chat thing. People act different when they can be anybody."

33

"That's juvenile," Lina scoffed, silently rationalizing her own behavior.

Alex lit a smoke and looked up at her. "Why?"

"Why?" Stalling . . .

"Oh, I remember. Because it's not *real life*."

"Well, that's true. It's not."

"Well, exactly. That's the whole point, right?"

Lina didn't want to tread that particular minefield with Alex. "So, who did *you* pretend to be?"

"I figured I'd just surf around a little bit, that's what Pete calls it, surfing around, but then I kind of got stuck in these rooms where people try to get you to have sex with them, just by writing back and forth. Didn't really do much for me. Maybe cos I'm a virgin." She looped her thumb under the strap of her black bikini top. "Am I getting a tan?"

Lina shifted her gaze to the pool. "You don't expect me to believe you're a virgin, do you?"

"Yeah, right." Alex smirked. "I mean online. Cybersex. Mindfucking. Drug of the twenty first century. The next best thing to being there."

"Why bother?"

"It's interesting to watch. Amazing what people will say when they're incognito. I went into a tarot room too. Too many people ahead of me to get my cards read, but supposedly it's not so bad late at night. Stargazer told me that. That's his screen name, Stargazer. At least I think he's a he. You never know, you know?"

"What a waste of time."

"What?"

"Fortune telling. It's absurd. And plebeian."

34

"Not into it, huh?"

"I don't abide by marching orders sent from cards or tea leaves or crystal balls."

"They're just guides."

"Reality's my guide. You should try it sometime."

Alex laid back and switched on her laptop. "Whatever floats your boat."

Lina turned and headed for the cabana. "And by the way," she called from the door, "tuna *is* fish." She swung the door closed behind her, but not before hearing the sound of Alex's computer dialing back online.

Lina lay in bed for half an hour but sleep eluded her. Every once in a while she'd hear Alex laughing outside, mimicking bird calls, humming. She tried to ignore it, but lying there with her eyes closed only made it seem louder and more directed at her. She finally gave in and decided to make better use of her time. She set out to straighten her Spartan and already immaculate room, but once the bathroom towels were refolded and aligned, distraction failed her. She went to the window's edge and peeked out. Alex was still busy with her laptop — probably breaking the blackjack bank, or maybe looking for love in the chat rooms.

She lifted the phone receiver and checked for a dial tone. There was none, and she felt the gauntlet of a challenge thrown before her. She scanned the floorboard to locate an outlet for the second phone line, and spotted it under her bed. Heart pounding, she plugged in her modem and dialed into the system. It seemed to take forever to connect, but finally the alluring palette of World CompuLine spread before her.

Perusing the icons, she clicked on her first order of business — CHANGE SCREEN NAME. She used her own name when writing to her father, but for other missions she always accepted the cloak of a nom de plume. She'd been PEGASUS, MISS ANTHROPE, WHRLGRL, ECHO . . . And now, faced with the empty box and a sense of adventure, she typed in her new identity: NXTDOOR.

Methodically, she switched into another section of the network and selected LOCATE A MEMBER ONLINE. It was a long shot, but the obvious place to start. She typed in Alex's name, and stared at the flashing hourglass until the reply appeared.

ALEX WILDER IS NOT SIGNED ON AT THIS TIME.

She tried every variation she could think of on the name, but no success. It was time for a tactical shift — travel to the front line. She pulled up the list of chat rooms and began scrolling. She suspected it would be quick and easy to narrow down where Alex might be lurking, but as the list continued to roll by, she realized she had her work cut out for her. It seemed almost all the rooms involved one type of sex or another, and she didn't really know Alex well enough to draw the fine lines demanded between such titles as HOT FEMS SEEKING STUD SERVICE, CUM

36

PLAY WITH ME, TRUTH OR DARE, TOYZ IN BABELAND, ALL THINGS KINKY, DUNGEON 4 DAMES, and eleven more full pages of similar inventory. Computer literate though she was, she would have to enlist help in this endeavor.

She studied the list and tried to find an innocuous place to enter the chat network. NEW MEMBER'S LOUNGE seemed the perfect choice. She connected into the room, then sat back and watched to determine the protocol. It seemed to be mostly an information forum, mixed with the excited ramblings of first-timers. She hoped to be able to glean some information without participating, but her plans were foiled when HPPYGOLCKY addressed her directly.

> HPPYGOLCKY: HEY NXTDOOR! SAW YOUR NAME
> POP UP ON OUR ROOM LIST. WELCOME!
> HERE'S A COFFEE 4 U. (_)⊃

She considered jumping to another room, but realized she could be tracked by her screen name and didn't want to invite pursuit. Besides, she wasn't ready to abort the mission just yet.

> NXTDOOR: THANK YOU, HPPY.
> HPPYGOLCKY: FIRST TIME ONLINE?
> NXTDOOR: NO. YOU?
> HPPYGOLCKY: BEEN ON OVER A YEAR. BUT
> STILL FINDING MY WAY AROUND.
> NXTDOOR: KNOW WHAT YOU MEAN. SLUMMING
> WITH THE NEOPHYTES?
> HPPYGOLCKY: ALWAYS LEARN NEW THINGS BY
> HELPING OTHER FOLKS.

ANGSTRDDN: HI ALL. BEEN 2 WKS 4 ME. ONLINE
    CONSTANTLY. SO MUCH TO CHOOSE FROM.
    MAKING ME CRAZY.
HPPYGOLCKY: SLOW DOWN, ANGST. HAVE A
    CIGARETTE ===≈
ANGSTRDDN: AHHHH, THANX . . . NEEDED THAT!
HARDBOD4U: HOT 27YO M HERE. ANYONE
    WANNA CHAT PRIVATE?
HPPYGOLCKY: WRONG ROOM, HARDBOD. TRY THE
    KINK LINK.
HARDBOD4U: DIDN'T SEE THAT ON THE LIST.
HPPYGOLCKY: ITS NOT. CLICK ON "KEYWORD"
    ICON, THEN TYPE "KINK LINK." YOU'LL BE
    THERE IN A FLASH.
HARDBOD4U: I'M OUTTA HERE!
ANGSTRDDN: KINK LINK, HUH . . .
HPPYGOLCKY: JUST HEARD OF IT. HAVEN'T BEEN
    THERE MYSELF.
ANGSTRDDN: I HAVE! UNBELIEVABLE!
    WHIPUHARD INVITED ME INTO A PRIVATE
    ROOM WITH LUVMSTRSS.
NXTDOOR: SPARE US THE DETAILS.
HPPYGOLCKY: ANGST, U M OR F?
ANGSTRDDN: M. 19. U?
HPPYGOLCKY: F. 25.
ANGSTRDDN: MMMM GOOD! NXTDOOR?

Lina panicked and considered signing off. She
certainly wasn't there to be cruised by adolescent
boys, but she wasn't there to be chased off by them
either.

NXTDOOR: M. 31.

ANGSTRDDN: TOO BAD. BUT I'VE GOT FIRST DIBS
    ON HPPY!!!
HPPYGPLCKY: NOT YOURS FOR THE DIBBING!
NXTDOOR: METHINKS THE LADY DOES NOT
    RETURN YOUR INTEREST.
ANGSTRDDN: GIVE ME TIME!
NXTDOOR: GET LOST.
ANGSTRDDN: HPPY, THAT WHAT U WANT???
HPPYGOLCKY: GOT THAT RIGHT!
ANGSTRDDN: HAVE IT YOUR WAY.
HPPYGOLCKY: THANKS, NXTDOOR.
NXTDOOR: YOU'RE WELCOME.
HPPYGOLCKY: U R A TRUE GENTLEMAN!

Lina wasn't quite sure how to respond to such a
compliment.

HPPYGOLCKY: PROBABLY BECAUSE YOU'RE
    OLDER. I FIND OLDER GUYS LESS ANNOYING
    IN GENERAL.
NXTDOOR: I KNOW WHAT YOU MEAN.
HPPYGOLCKY: SO, WHAT'RE U INTO?

Stalling . . .

NXTDOOR: WITH RESPECT TO WHAT?
HPPYGOLCKY: WHAT R U LOOKING FOR ONLINE?
    WE'RE ALL HERE 4 SOMETHING!
NXTDOOR: I'M LOOKING FOR SOMEONE.
HPPYGOLCKY: AREN'T WE ALL!!!
NXTDOOR: SOMEONE IN PARTICULAR.
HPPYGOLCKY: WHO?
NXTDOOR: NOT AT LIBERTY TO SAY.

HPPYGOLCKY: GOT IT. WHAT'RE THEY INTO?

NXTDOOR: SEX ROOMS.

HPPYGOLCKY: THAT DOESN'T NARROW IT DOWN
MUCH.

NXTDOOR: I NOTICED.

HPPYGOLCKY: WHAT KIND OF SEX?

NXTDOOR: DON'T KNOW HER THAT WELL.

HPPYGOLCKY: BUT YOU WANT TO . . .

NXTDOOR: OLD FRIEND. JUST HEARD SHE WAS
ONLINE AND HOPED TO RECONNECT.

HPPYGOLCKY: WHO SAW HER ONLINE?

Lina wasn't sure where this was leading or how
to get around it, but she had to think fast.

NXTDOOR: STARGAZER.

HPPYGOLCKY: HAVE U ASKED STARGAZER
WHERE YOUR FRIEND WAS ONLINE AND
WHAT NAME SHE WAS USING?

That route hadn't even occurred to her. She'd
forgotten about Stargazer until the moment she
blurted it out.

NXTDOOR: WHY DIDN'T I THINK OF THAT?

HPPYGOLCKY: MAYBE U WERE DESTINED TO
COME IN HERE AND MEET ME . . .

Lina was ready to jump out of the room right
then and get on STARGAZER's track. But that would
certainly violate protocol.

HPPYGOLCKY: <--- SINGLE. AVAILABLE. R U?

```
NXTDOOR: <--- FLATTERED, BUT NEITHER.
HPPYGOLCKY: OH WELL . . . U CAN'T BLAME A
    GIRL 4 TRYING!
NXTDOOR: NO, YOU CAN'T.
MARK100: TRYING WHAT?
HPPYGOLCKY: AH, WE HAVE A NEW ROOMMATE.
    HI MARK.
MARK100: MY FRIEND LONERNGR IS HERE TOO. I
    THINK.
LONERNGR: RIGHT HERE. HOWDY ALL.
```

Lina capitalized on the fresh blood to make her exit.

```
NXTDOOR: TIME FOR ME TO BID YOU ALL ADIEU.
    THANKS FOR YOUR HELP, HPPY.
HPPYGOLCKY: PLEASURE WAS MINE.
MARK100: WAIT, NXTDOOR. U F OR M?
NXTDOOR: M. 31.
MARK100: SEE YA.
NXTDOOR: GOOD-BYE.
```

Lina exited the room and selected the command LOCATE A MEMBER ONLINE. With a mix of excitement and trepidation, she typed in STARGAZER and cast her line into the cyber-sea.

The hourglass began to flash, and in a moment, she got her first bite.

STARGAZER IS IN CRYSTAL BALL FORUM.

She quickly switched back to the list of rooms and scrolled through the full eleven pages, but there

was no such listing. That was impossible. Unless . . .
She clicked the KEYWORD icon and typed in CRYSTAL
BALL.

WELCOME TO THE CRYSTAL BALL FORUM.

A car motor revved suddenly outside, and she
craned to look out the window. Alex was backing out
of the driveway in the Lexus, or trying to. Lina
quickly turned off the computer and dashed outside.
"Hello . . ." She waved to halt her. "Wait a minute,
please."

Alex leaned her head out the window. "Yeah?"

Lina approached as quickly as she could with no
breath left and trying to appear composed. "I need to
use this car."

"Me too." Alex grinned. "Mine's in the shop. Dirt
in the motor or something."

"No, I mean I have to go pick up Sean from class
in just a few minutes."

"Whaddaya think I'm doing?"

"Excuse me?"

"I'm on my way to get him. Gotta spend some
time with the little bro'. Sisterliness, you know?" She
winked.

Lina sensed a scheme, but had no authority to
stop her. "Very well then. Do you know where the
class is held?"

"Hell no, I figured I'd just ride around downtown
yelling his name out the window." Alex shifted into
reverse and started backing up. "Maybe hang a few
posters. Milk cartons . . ." She screeched into the

road. "Nothing's too good for my bro'!" She peeled off down the street. Lina ducked under a spray of pebbles, and wondered how she could be attracted to someone so vile.

5

Lina gently set needle to phonograph and filled the living room with Vivaldi's "Four Seasons." Usually she and Sean would be at the Video Jones arcade right now. He'd be perched on the green booster stool he used to reach the machines, begging for just one more quarter. She figured he'd probably ask Alex to take him there, but surely her newborn sisterliness would quickly grow old.

Having made it only through "Spring," she abandoned Vivaldi and wandered into the kitchen. With Claire and Nathan at a Bar Association function, it would be just she and Sean for dinner. She pulled open the restaurant-sized freezer and stared in. She'd make cheeseburgers and fries, Sean's favorite. She tossed a pound of ground beef into the microwave to defrost while she sliced the potatoes. Sean preferred his burgers square, so she sculpted two cubes and flattened them on the grill. Reconsidering, she added a third. Alex would probably insist on joining them just to spite her, espousing some convoluted rationale for why cheeseburgers weren't meat.

But when Sean finally trotted into the house, with a chocolate tomato sauce smile, Lina realized dinner was off.

"We had pizza!" he squealed.

She stooped to wipe his face. "And chocolate, from the looks of it."

"Almond Joy!"

"I never knew you liked Almond Joys."

"Sometimes you feel like a nut." He giggled and shrugged. "Sometimes you don't."

Alex danced in the door behind him, bellowing. "Almond Joy's got nuts, Mounds don't. Because . . ." She motioned to him in cue.

"Sometimes you feel like a nut, sometimes you don't." He doubled over in laughter, then poked Alex in the belly and charged for the stairs. "You're it!"

He made it up five steps before Alex grabbed him by the ankles and felled him. "Am not!" She tickled him. "Say it!" He shimmied free of her, and she scrambled after him on all fours. Her shirt hung loose as she climbed, and Lina caught sight of the black bikini peeking out from underneath. When she reached the top, Alex kneeled on the landing, out of breath. The shadows carved her high cheekbones even higher, and the white oxford draped off her shoulders and dipped to a "Y" between her breasts. She stared down at Lina, and though the house was dead quiet, she whispered. "You're it."

Lina searched Alex's eyes for innuendo. Was this woman flirting with her? Or was she the type whose unaimed sensuality ricocheted everywhere — causing casualties without claiming them? Either way, Lina knew she was in trouble. And then she smelled smoke . . .

It was just a tiny fire. A sliver of orange dancing across the backs of three charred squares. It burned itself out before Lina could even decide what to throw on it, but the smell of burnt grease still wafted through the house. She opened the side door to draw a cross breeze, then used a spatula to scrape the burgers off the grill and poke them down the garbage disposal. She heard bath water running upstairs, and realized Alex was preparing Sean for bed. Apparently she was no longer needed that night.

Headlights streaked across the bedroom wall and then went dark. Lina could hear the click of Claire's heels stumbling across the driveway, then Nathan's voice.

"Watch out for the steps."

"Don't be silly, darling," Claire reassured just before tumbling into an azalea bush.

Lina watched from the window. It wasn't often that Claire drank anymore, but when she did it was still to excess. Nathan helped Claire to her feet.

"Let's go peek in on the baby," she slurred.

"He's not a baby, dear. And I'm sure Lina has everything under control."

"Yes, but I'm his mother." Claire rummaged through her purse. "There's no replacing a mother."

"You're right, of course," Nathan acquiesced.

Claire dumped her bag onto the porch. "I can't find my keys."

Nathan jingled the keys in front of her face. "I drove. Remember?"

Claire giggled. "Silly me."

"Let me give you a hand." Lina came around the side of the pool and joined them on the porch. "How was the party?" She stooped to collect Claire's belongings.

Nathan was visibly relieved. "Very enjoyable, thank you."

"It wasn't a party, darling." Claire motioned for Nathan to unlock the door. "It was a meeting. Important people doing important things that impact the entire community." She gleamed with pride. "Isn't that right?"

Nathan took her by the arm and hustled her into the foyer. "Yes, dear."

She took several steps down the hall, then stopped abruptly and spun around. "I smell smoke. Has Alex been smoking in the house again? I've told her a hundred times not to smoke in the house."

"Not that I know of..." Lina hedged. "But I'll talk with her about it in the morning."

"Thank you, dear. You're such a blessing. I wish Alex were more like you."

I don't think so, Lina thought. "It's no problem." She forced a smile.

"I'm going up to check on the baby." Claire grabbed the banister and pulled herself up several steps. "There's no replacing a mother, you know."

Lina nodded. "That's true."

"Oh . . . I'm sorry, darling . . ." Claire blanched. "How insensitive of me."

"Please, don't worry. It's fine." Lina assured. "I'm sure he'll be happy to know you're home."

"Yes. I'm sure he will." She disappeared up the stairs.

Nathan loosened his tie. "You were up late last night."

"Excuse me?" Lina quickly busied herself collecting the remainder of Claire's belongings.

"Your lights were on when I got up this morning."

"Oh, right. I had a paper due today." She laid Claire's belongings on the credenza. "I just wanted it to be perfect."

"Serious and ambitious." He smiled in his fatherly way. "As I've noted before."

"Yes, sir. Thank you."

"Alex hasn't been interfering . . ." He raised his brow. "Keeping you from your work?"

"Oh no, not at all. She keeps to herself mostly."

"Don't be offended." He chuckled and started up the stairs. "That's just how she is. A bit gruff on the exterior, but she has a good heart."

"Yes sir, I'm sure she does." Lina switched off the hall lights and stepped out onto the porch.

"Try to get some sleep," he called.

"Of course. Goodnight." She pulled the front door closed behind her.

* * * * *

A full and yellow moon hung low in the sky, and Lina worked by its light so as not to draw attention. Curled crossed-legged against the bay window, computer on her lap, she clicked the KEYWORD icon and typed in CRYSTAL BALL. She stared out across the pool as the hourglass flashed. Alex was stretched belly down across her bed, pillow wedged beneath her chest, cigarette dangling from her lips . . . the full, pouty kind of lips that always drove Lina crazy. Alex's laptop was propped in front of her, and from time to time she'd type, smile, puff her cigarette. Lina tried to remember what she used to do at night before Alex came home. She couldn't.

WELCOME TO THE CRYSTAL BALL FORUM.

Lina was in, and hunting season was on. She leaned back against the cool window pane and stared at the glowing screen.

KIZMET: THAT'S NOT WHAT I MEANT.
PLAYGRL: WHAT DID U MEAN, THEN?
NITECRONE: HE MEANT THAT TIME IS THE
    SAME THING AS MOTION. NEITHER
    CONSTRUCT EXISTS WITHOUT THE OTHER.
KIZMET: NO, I MEANT THAT BECAUSE THEY ARE
    CONSTRUCTS, NEITHER REALLY EXISTS AT
    ALL.
RUSHIN: SO THEY'RE METAPHENOMENAL.
PLAYGRL: U R METAPHENOMENAL!
RUSHIN: <--- JUST PLAIN PHENOMENAL!!!

KIZMET: NO, THEY'RE PHENOMENOLOGICAL
    ARTIFACTS.
PLAYGRL: LOOSEN UP, KIZ.
ANARKIST: YEAH, IT'S ALL BULLSHIT ANYWAY.
    NONE OF US EVEN REALLY EXIST, RIGHT?
NITECRONE: <--- EXISTS!
RUSHIN: <--- EXISTS!
PLAYGRL: <--- EXISTS!
ANARKIST: <--- ARTIFACT.

Lina had little to contribute to any discussion of
metaphysics — at least nothing that wouldn't
immediately expose her as a disbeliever. But the
digression opened a door for her to jump in.

NXTDOOR: <--- UNDECIDED.
NITECRONE: WELCOME TO OUR DOMAIN,
    NXTDOOR.
ANARKIST: YOU M OR F?
NXTDOOR: M, 31. AND YOU?
ANARKIST: 27/M.
PLAYGRL: <--- F, 20.
KIZMET: M29
NITECRONE: F/45.
ANARKIST: 45 AND A CRONE?
NITECRONE: ASPIRING . . .
RUSHIN: F. AGELESS. TIME'S AN ARTIFACT,
    RIGHT?
NITECRONE: IF ONLY. U MUST BE YOUNG.
RUSHIN: <--- MAGICIAN. NEWBORN CHILD OF
    THE DIVINE.
PLAYGRL: <--- JUST PLAIN DIVINE!
NITECRONE: U KNOW THE TAROT, RUSHIN?
RUSHIN: DABBLE A BIT.

PLAYGRL: ME 2. GOT A READING IN HERE
    EARLIER FROM STARGAZER. BLEW ME AWAY.

Lina's heart pounded. She lifted her scope and took aim.

NXTDOOR: YOU KNOW STARGAZER?
PLAYGRL: JUST KNOW HE DOES READINGS.
NITECRONE: HE'S A SHE. SHE'S IN HERE MOST
    NIGHTS, SOMETIMES IN "NAKED TAROT."
NXTDOOR: NAKED TAROT?
NITECRONE: PRIVATE ROOM. LOTS OF READERS
    HANG OUT THERE. TALK SHOP.
PLAYGRL: AWESOME! ANYONE WANNA GO?
NXTDOOR: I'M GAME.
NITECRONE: <--- PREFERS TO REMAIN CLOTHED.
RUSHIN: COUNT ME IN!
ANARKIST: GOING WHERE THE WOMEN GO . . . IF
    U DON'T MIND THE COMPETITION,
    NXTDOOR???
NXTDOOR: <--- DOESN'T HAVE ANY.
PLAYGRL: TOUCHE. LIKE YOUR STYLE, NXTDOOR.
NXTDOOR: :::BOWING TO THE LADY:::
RUSHIN: ENOUGH YOU TWO! LETS GO.
PLAYGRL: SEE YOU THERE.
NXTDOOR: RIGHT BEHIND YOU.

Lina clicked on the PRIVATE ROOM icon and typed in NAKED TAROT. The screen went blank, then quickly refilled.

LTTLDVL: BUT WHICH JOB SHOULD I TAKE?
4TUNETLLR: THE CHOICE ISN'T WHAT'S
    IMPORTANT. MAKING IT IS. YOU'VE GOT THE

INFORMATION YOU NEED. SEARCH YOURSELF
FEARLESSLY.

LTTLDVL: I THOUGHT YOU'RE SUPPOSED TO
TELL ME MY FUTURE.

RUSHIN: OTHERS CAN POINT TO PATHS. U
GOTTA WALK YOURSELF.

4TUNETLLR: WELL SAID.

RUSHIN: <--- WANTS READING.

4TUNETLLR: GREETINGS, RUSHIN. SOULSEEKR
WILL PUT U IN QUEUE. ASTRAEA IS UP
NEXT, THEN LONGSFFRNG, SHAKTI, AND
NEWTON.

SOULSEEKR: U R WELCOME TO STAY AND
OBSERVE. OR U CAN GO 2 ANOTHER ROOM
AND WE'LL I.M. U WHEN IT'S YOUR TURN.

RUSHIN: I.M.?

ANARKIST: INSTANT MESSAGE. U CAN SEND ONE
TO ANYONE IN ANY ROOM. GOES DIRECTLY
TO THEIR SCREEN ONLY. TOTALLY PRIVATE.

RUSHIN: AWESOME. HOW DOES IT WORK?

ANARKIST: CLICK ON "MEMBERS" ICON. CHOOSE
"SEND INSTANT MESSAGE." TYPE IN
PERSON'S NAME AND YOUR MESSAGE. HIT
"SEND." VOILA!

ASTRAEA: HEY, CAN I GET MY READING NOW?

4TUNETLLR: VERY WELL. LET'S CONTINUE.

Lina quickly moved her cursor to the MEMBERS
icon and double clicked. She didn't want to get stuck
in a room she couldn't talk in. Not with Alex right
there. She selected INSTANT MESSAGE, and typed
PLAYGRL.

NXTDOOR: ARE YOU GOING TO STAY IN HERE?

She hesitated briefly, then hit SEND. She imagined the message traveling out the window, across the pool, into the bedroom that used to be hers. Alex was perched at the head of her bed now, laptop between her legs. And she was typing. As accomplished as Lina was with the computer, this capture was surely her best work yet . . .

But as the minutes passed without reply, Lina began to wonder if she hadn't miscalculated, violated protocol, stepped out on a limb that wouldn't support her. To break the fall, she told herself it was for the best. She had no business pursuing Alex this way, or any other. It only complicated matters and reflected a total lack of self discipline, which she loathed. But the rationalization was a Band-Aid — thinly pasted and quickly shed when the green-bordered box lit up her screen.

PLAYGRL: TELL ME IF U GET THIS. THINK I'M
    PUSHING THE WRONG BUTTONS OR
    SOMETHING.
NXTDOOR: YOU'VE MADE IT.
PLAYGRL: :::RELIEF::: AFRAID YOU'D THINK I WAS
    BLOWING U OFF.
NXTDOOR: NEVER.
PLAYGRL: ANARKIST SENT ME AN I.M. TOO.
NXTDOOR: DOESN'T SURPRISE ME.
PLAYGRL: ASKED IF I'D GET HIM OFF BEFORE
    HIS WIFE GOT HOME.
NXTDOOR: HOW ROMANTIC.
PLAYGRL: TOTALLY UNCOUTH. DIDN'T RESPOND.

NXTDOOR: <--- VERY COUTH.
PLAYGRL: I CAN TELL. AND ROMANTIC?
NXTDOOR: SURE. ASK ANY OF MY EX'S...
PLAYGRL: LOL. U SAY EX'S, NOT GIRLFRIEND...
    LOVER...WIFE...
NXTDOOR: WHAT'S "LOL"?
PLAYGRL: LAUGHING OUT LOUD. IT'S STANDARD
    CYBER-LINGO. U NEW ONLINE?
NXTDOOR: IN A WAY.
PLAYGRL: INTERESTING. BUT WE DIGRESS...
NXTDOOR: INDEED.
PLAYGRL: SO, R U SPOKEN FOR?
NXTDOOR: NOT REALLY.
PLAYGRL: IS THAT A NO OR A YES BUT?
NXTDOOR: IT'S A NO.
PLAYGRL: HMMMM.
NXTDOOR: WHAT...?
PLAYGRL: WHAT R U WEARING?

Lina stared down at her silk nightshirt and tattered moccasins, and tried to ignore that the conversation had just taken a huge turn.

NXTDOOR: JEANS. WHITE SHIRT. GREEN DOC
    MARTENS, UNLACED.
PLAYGRL: MMMMM. A CASUAL MAN. AND
    MYSTERIOUS...
NXTDOOR: MYSTERIOUS?
PLAYGRL: I LOOKED U UP IN THE MEMBERS
    DIRECTORY WHEN I GOT YOUR I.M. U HAVE
    NO PROFILE.
NXTDOOR: :::TURNING SIDEWAYS TO CHECK:::
PLAYGIRL: LOL! A PROFILE IS WHERE U WRITE

THINGS ABOUT YOURSELF, THEN POST IT. IT
ATTRACTS PEOPLE TO YOU.
NXTDOOR: HOW?
PLAYGRL: SHARED INTERESTS. PHYSICAL
DESCRIPTION. PROXIMITY.
NXTDOOR: DO YOU HAVE ONE?
PLAYGRL: SURE. IT'S OPTIONAL, BUT LOTS OF
PEOPLE WON'T TALK TO YOU IF U DON'T
HAVE ONE.
NXTDOOR: I WANT TO READ IT.
PLAYGRL: CLICK "MEMBERS" ICON, CHOOSE
"READ PROFILE", TYPE "PLAYGRL."
NXTDOOR: I'LL BE RIGHT BACK. DON'T GO AWAY.
PLAYGRL: DON'T WORRY.

While Lina called up the profile, she tried to
mentally compose her own. It would have to look
perfect if it was to serve as her passport in this land.
A delicate balance of fact and fiction. Alex's would,
no doubt, resemble a sports car entangled in
artemisia.

SCREEN NAME: PLAYGRL
FULL NAME: KELLY H.
LOCATION: FREEPORT, ME
BIRTH DATE: ANNO DOMINI
MARITAL STATUS: HAPPILY SINGLE
COMPUTER: OBVIOUSLY
OCCUPATION: DANCER, RIVER RAFT GUIDE
HOBBIES: HIKING, FURNITURE MAKING, META-
PHYSICS
PERSONAL QUOTE: LIFE IS A BANQUET . . . EAT
WITH YOUR FINGERS!

Lina panicked and considered signing off. She reminded herself of Alex's proclamation that everyone lied about everything online, and tried to fight the sinking feeling that she might be talking to someone else.

NXTDOOR: I'M BACK.
PLAYGRL: SO, WHADDYA THINK?
NXTDOOR: I ADMIT IT PIQUED MY INTEREST.
PLAYGRL: MISSION ACCOMPLISHED.
NXTDOOR: SO YOU R 20, IF I RECALL FROM
    EARLIER?
PLAYGRL: RIGHT-O! MATURE FOR MY AGE, OF
    COURSE.
NXTDOOR: STUDENT?
PLAYGRL: STUDENT OF LIFE! STUDIED AT UCLA
    FOR A YEAR, BUT MISSED THE CHANGE OF
    SEASONS AND MOVED BACK HERE. STARTED
    DANCING AND NEVER FINISHED MY DEGREE.
    THAT A PROBLEM?

Huge problem, which Lina couldn't begin to explain.

NXTDOOR: OF COURSE NOT.
PLAYGRL: SOME PEOPLE ARE HUNG UP ON THE
    IDEA OF SCHOOL. LIKE IT'S THE ONLY WAY
    TO EDUCATE YOURSELF. LIKE ALL OF LIFE
    ISN'T ONE BIG LESSON.
NXTDOOR: I KNOW WHAT YOU MEAN. SO, WHAT
    TYPE OF DANCING DO YOU DO?
PLAYGRL: EXOTIC. WANNA COME TO A SHOW
    SOMETIME?
NXTDOOR: <--- FAR AWAY FROM FREEPORT.

PLAYGRL: AND I THOUGHT U WERE NEXT-DOOR.

So did I, Lina thought. She looked out across the pool. Alex's room was dark.

PLAYGRL: SO TELL ME ABOUT U.
NXTDOOR: SUCH AS?
PLAYGRL: WHERE ARE U?
NXTDOOR: SEATTLE.
PLAYGRL: I'VE HIKED ON MT. BAKER.
NXTDOOR: SO HAVE I.
PLAYGRL: WHAT DO U LOOK LIKE?

Lina chuckled at the irony and considered bowing out of the conversation — but it *was* a good opportunity to take the "M/31" profile for a test run. If she ever did find Alex, it would serve her well to be as prepared as possible.

NXTDOOR: 6'2". BLACK HAIR. BROWN EYES.
PLAYGRL: <--- 5'7". DARK BROWN HAIR, WAVY.
    BLUE EYES, BIG. CONSIDERED CUTE BY MOST
    GUYS.
NXTDOOR: I BELIEVE THAT.
PLAYGRL: R U LIKE MOST GUYS?
NXTDOOR: PROBABLY, IN SOME WAYS.
PLAYGRL: DO U FIND ME ATTRACTIVE?
NXTDOOR: JUDGING BY YOUR FONT ...
PLAYGRL: LOL. WANT MY GIF?
NXTDOOR: GIF???
PLAYGRL: PHOTO. U CAN SCAN PICTURES INTO
    YOUR COMPUTER, THEN SEND THEM
    AROUND THROUGH E-MAIL.
NXTDOOR: WHY?

PLAYGRL: PEOPLE LIKE TO SEE WHAT U LOOK
    LIKE.
NXTDOOR: YOU COULD SCAN IN ANY PHOTO AND
    SAY IT WAS YOU.
PLAYGRL: HAPPENS ALL THE TIME. MY PAL
    SHEDONISM HAD HER OWN GIF SENT BACK
    TO HER ONCE BY A GUY WANTING A
    THREESOME. HE SAID IT WAS HIS WIFE.
NXTDOOR: HOW'D HE GET HOLD OF IT?
PLAYGRL: THOSE THINGS GET PASSED AROUND
    ONCE U PUT THEM OUT THERE.
NXTDOOR: <--- NOT PUBLIC DOMAIN.
PLAYGRL: I RESPECT THAT.
NXTDOOR: IS YOUR GIF REALLY YOU?
PLAYGRL: U BET. NO FALSE ADVERTISING HERE.
NXTDOOR: SEND IT. BUT NOT TILL AFTER WE'RE
    DONE TALKING. O.K.?
PLAYGRL: AGREED. U PREFER TO IMAGINE?
NXTDOOR: I SEE YOU THROUGH YOUR WORDS.
PLAYGRL: A POET . . .
NXTDOOR: NEVER BEEN ACCUSED OF THAT.
PLAYGRL: A LOVER?
NXTDOOR: TO SOME.
PLAYGRL: TO ME?

Things moved quickly here in cyberspace. Lina
didn't feel ready, but a certain wetness betrayed her.

PLAYGRL: STILL THERE?
NXTDOOR: STILL HERE.
PLAYGRL: NERVOUS?
NXTDOOR: SHY.

PLAYGRL: THEN ALLOW ME. :::CROSSING TOWARD
U . . . UNBUTTONING YOUR SHIRT . . . TOO
TIGHT AROUND YOUR NECK . . . U NEED TO
BREATHE:::

A moment passed before PLAYGRL continued. Her
pauses set a' rhythm.

PLAYGRL: :::LOOSENING YOUR BELT . . . MY ARM
BRUSHES AGAINST YOUR CROTCH . . . SLIDING
YOUR SHIRT OFF YOUR SHOULDERS . . . U
FEEL MY NAILS:::
NXTDOOR: YES.
PLAYGRL: R U HOT?
NXTDOOR: VERY.
PLAYGRL: KISS ME THEN.
NXTDOOR: :::PLACING MY HANDS ON YOUR
FACE . . . RUBBING MY LIPS ACROSS YOURS . . .
GENTLY:::
PLAYGRL: :::SLIDING TWO FINGERS IN YOUR
MOUTH . . . PULLING YOUR LIPS AGAINST
MINE . . . WANT TO TASTE U:::
NXTDOOR: :::KISSING YOU . . . MOVING MY BODY
AGAINST YOURS:::
PLAYGRL: :::MOVING WITH U . . . HOLDING U
CLOSE:::
NXTDOOR: :::LIFTING YOUR SHIRT . . . TRACING MY
FINGERTIPS ACROSS THE LACE OF YOUR
BRA . . . SLIDING IT DOWN TO REVEAL THE
FULLNESS OF YOUR BREASTS:::
PLAYGRL: :::SLIDING A HAND BEHIND YOUR
NECK . . . URGING YOUR LIPS TO MY NIPPLES:::

NXTDOOR: :::LICKING . . . NIBBLING . . . KISSING . . .
ROLLING YOUR NIPPLE BETWEEN MY ⌐IPS:::
PLAYGRL: U R MAKING ME WET . . .
NXTDOOR: :::SLIDING MY HAND BETWEEN YOUR
LEGS . . . HOT . . . VERY HOT:::
PLAYGRL: :::MOVING AGAINST YOUR HAND:::
NXTDOOR: :::KISSING MY WAY DOWN THE CURVE
OF YOUR BELLY . . . UNZIPPING YOUR
PANTS . . . SLIDING THEM DOWN . . . LOOKING
AT YOU:::
PLAYGRL: I FEEL YOUR EYES ON ME . . .
NXTDOOR: :::BRUSHING MY LIPS UP THE INSIDE
OF YOUR THIGHS . . . RUNNING MY TONGUE
ALONG THE EDGE OF YOUR PANTIES . . .
TASTING THE CURL OF YOUR HAIR . . . YOUR
SCENT:::
PLAYGRL: I AM SOAKING . . .
NXTDOOR: :::LICKING YOU THROUGH YOUR
PANTIES . . . HOT . . . DAMP AGAINST MY
CHEEKS . . . BITING AT THE FABRIC . . .
PULLING IT ASIDE:::
PLAYGRL: WANT TO FEEL YOUR MOUTH . . .
NXTDOOR: :::PARTING YOUR LIPS WITH MY
TONGUE . . . LICKING SLOWLY . . . ALONG EVERY
FOLD OF SKIN:::
PLAYGRL: :::ROCKING AGAINST YOUR FACE . . .
WETNESS SLIDING OVER U . . . MY HANDS IN
YOUR HAIR . . . PULLING U CLOSE:::
NXTDOOR: :::DIPPING . . . DARTING . . . CIRCLING
YOUR CLIT . . . SLIDING A FINGER INSIDE
YOU . . . THEN ANOTHER:::

PLAYGRL: :::TIGHTENING AROUND YOUR FINGERS
... SQUEEZING ... PULSING:::
NXTDOOR: :::FOLLOWING YOUR MOTION ...
PULLING YOU TOWARD ME FROM INSIDE:::
PLAYGRL: HEADING OVER THE EDGE ...
NXTDOOR: :::TONGUE PRESSING YOUR CLIT ...
RELEASING ... PRESSING AGAIN ... THRUSTING
INSIDE YOU ... DEEPER ... DEEPER:::
PLAYGRL: !*#@!!**%$!
NXTDOOR: :::WET LIPS CURLING INTO A GRIN:::
PLAYGRL: <--- PUDDLED
NXTDOOR: REALLY ...
PLAYGRL: SERIOUSLY!
NXTDOOR: SERIOUSLY PUDDLED ...
PLAYGRL: WAS HAVING A HARD TIME TYPING
WITH ONE HAND ...
NXTDOOR: LOL!
PLAYGRL: :-) <--- SIDEWAYS GRIN
NXTDOOR: SO, IS THIS WHERE WE SMOKE?
PLAYGRL: <--- ALREADY SMOKIN'!!!
NXTDOOR: GLAD TO HEAR IT. AIM TO PLEASE.
PLAYGRL: A TRUE LADIES' MAN!
NXTDOOR: MUST ADD THAT TO MY VITAE.
PLAYGRL: <--- HAPPY TO SERVE AS A
REFERENCE! SURE YOU HAVE PLENTY
ALREADY.
NXTDOOR: LEGIONS ... :-)
PLAYGRL: U DO THIS A LOT?
NXTDOOR: FIRST TIME.
PLAYGRL: NO WAY ...
NXTDOOR: WAY.

PLAYGRL: HOT DAMN!!! U R SOMETHING ELSE!

"If you only knew *how* 'something else'..."

NXTDOOR: THANKS. SO ARE YOU.
PLAYGRL: SO...
NXTDOOR: YES?
PLAYGRL: NOW THAT WE'VE FUCKED...
NXTDOOR: YES?
PLAYGRL: WHAT'S YOUR NAME?

Lina glanced around the room and spotted her Abnormal Psychology book on her desk. *A Mind for Deviance* by Zachary Banyon.

NXTDOOR: MY NAME IS ZACHARY. BUT MY
    FRIENDS CALL ME...WELL...ZACHARY.
PLAYGRL: GOTTA LOVE IT! A GUY THAT CAN
    SCREW U AND MAKE U LAUGH!
NXTDOOR: IT'S BEEN A PLEASURE.
PLAYGRL: THE PLEASURE WAS ALL MINE,
    ZACHARY...

As Lina crawled into bed that night, cool sheets collapsing against the sweat of her skin, she knew some of the pleasure had been hers. She slipped a hand between her legs, and massaged herself beyond the ache...and into sleep.

6

The seven a.m. sun split the morning fog and glared triumphantly into Lina's puffed and blood-shot eyes. "*Merde*..." She squinted and tried to round the pool half-blind. There was no point trying to grab another half-hour of sleep. She was exhausted, but she was awake.

A wall of refrigerated air greeted her as she stepped into the foyer. Goose bumps spread up her bare arms and legs, and she rubbed her skirt against her thighs for warmth. The house was quiet, and she hopscotched the cedar floorboards on tiptoe to avoid creaking. Alex's door was cracked open, and she veered toward it on impulse, declining to analyze her motivations so early in the morning.

Oblivious to the sunlight pouring through her window, Alex lay curled like a sleeping kitten — white sheet twisted around her torso and tucked between tan legs, red-streaked hair wrapped over her face and shoulders, lips parted slightly. An image impossible not to commit to memory, though Lina knew she'd regret it.

"Why do you have your booties on?" Sean sat cross-legged in the corner of the room, in his underwear. Lina stifled a gasp. How could she have missed him?

"Whoa..." Alex got her first blast of sunlight. She rolled over and propped herself up on one elbow. "What's up?" She eyed her visitors.

"I just... peeked in... to look for Sean," Lina stuttered. "He wasn't in his room, and I was worried... and then I saw your door was open... and I thought he might be in here... with you." She heard herself rambling but couldn't stop. "And he was... I mean, he is. See." She motioned to Sean.

"I was waiting for the big hand to get to the six." He held out his Super Mario watch. "And I was being quiet!"

"Where are your pajamas?" Lina's hands went to her hips.

"Don't wear any." Alex cocked her head coyly.

"I meant... him." Lina blushed, knowing Alex was toying with her.

"She said I didn't need them." Sean pointed at Alex.

"Guilty." Alex held the sheet against her chest and sat up. "You wear clothes to bed?"

Lina didn't care to discuss bed with Alex. "That's irrelevant." She motioned for Sean. "Let's get some clothes on you before your mother sees you."

Sean stood. "Why do you have your booties on?"

Lina looked down at her feet and was mortified to see her moccasins.

"She's making a statement." Alex smirked. "It says, 'I'm a woman of many sides . . . don't expect consistency from me.'"

Lina stepped back into the hall. "It says I was only half-awake when I dressed this morning. Let's go." She nodded to Sean.

"We're going to an outing." He shuffled toward her.

"Excuse me?" Lina looked past him to Alex.

"I told him I'd take him on an outing today if the weather was nice." Alex wrapped her sheet around her and crossed to the window. "The weather's nice . . ." She tilted her head back and closed her eyes.

"You could come!" Sean took Lina's hand and turned to Alex. "Couldn't Lina come?"

"Of course," Alex replied without opening her eyes.

Lina tugged Sean toward the stairway. "We'll discuss it while you're getting dressed," she bribed, knowing it was out of the question.

As the Lexus screeched backwards into the street,

Lina fastened her seat belt and cursed herself for letting Alex drive. "There's a child in the car," she reminded sternly.

Alex slid her Ray-Bans on and popped a CD into the disk player. "No problem." She cracked open her window and lit a cigarette. "First one of the day's always the tastiest!" She exhaled sideways through a grin. Lina opened her window and leaned her head out. Alex reached and tapped the Camels against her thigh. "Want one?"

Lina looked down at Alex's hand. "No."

"Good guardianship of your vehicle!" Alex gave a thumbs up.

"Excuse me?"

"Your bio-vehicle." She squeezed Lina's bare leg. "This material your spirit chose to manifest in."

"You mean my body?"

"Well, secularly speaking, yes." She turned to Lina and lifted her Ray-Bans. "I mean your body."

Lina struggled under the weight of Alex's gaze. She suddenly couldn't remember what they were talking about.

"You vegetarian?" Alex slid her glasses back down and returned her hand to the wheel.

"No." Lina turned to her. "And neither are you."

"No shit!" Alex puffed her smoke. "I just enjoy throwing Claire over the edge."

"She said 'shit!' " Sean chimed from the back seat. Lina glared at Alex. "And Mom said don't call her that." He wagged his finger. "She doesn't like it."

"Exactly." Alex turned up the music and belted along with Annie Lennox.

* * * * *

Sean chased geese up and down a nearby hill while Alex and Lina unloaded the car.

"You look three fries short of a 'Happy Meal!' " Alex smacked Lina on the arm with a rolled up newspaper.

Lina turned to her with a most serious expression. "I was *wondering* what someone like you would be doing with a newspaper. I should've known."

"Ha-ha." Alex tucked the paper under her arm. "It just so happens that I brought it to read."

"Oh, she reads!" Lina heaved the ice chest from the trunk.

"How butch of you . . ." Alex smirked. "It doesn't match with the skirt, though."

"I'm a woman of many sides." Lina started off toward Sean. "Don't expect consistency from me."

Alex grabbed a blanket and chased after her. "Anyone ever tell you you've got a mean streak?"

Lina trudged up the hill and ignored her.

The sun was directly overhead as they finished the last of the watermelon. Lina busied herself tugging at pieces of grass, as Alex licked her sticky fingers. "That was great! Cold and sweet." Alex wiped her lips. "Melts in your mouth like nothing else in this world!" She winked.

More innuendo? Lina wouldn't take the bait. "Yes. It was delicious." Alex looked disappointed. Or maybe Lina just wished she did. "As for you . . ." Lina reached and tickled Sean's bare feet. "I believe a nap is in order."

"I'm not sleepy!" He leapt up. "I want to ride the swings!"

"You rode the swings all morning."

"But I'm not finished. I want my feet to get up to the sun." He turned to Alex. "You could come push me!"

"Not right now, little boy." She laid back against a tree. "I'm gonna plant my butt right here and read the paper." She shot a glance at Lina.

Sean giggled. "She said 'butt!' "

"Come on." Lina stood. "Five minutes on the swing, and then a nap."

"Fifteen!" He countered with big eyes.

"Ten." She took his hand. It always weighed in his favor that he reminded her of herself.

Twenty minutes later, Lina carried Sean back up the hill on piggy-back. Satisfied and exhausted from touching his feet to the sun, he curled up on the blanket and quickly fell asleep.

"It was fun to watch you with him." Alex spoke from behind her paper. "Nice, I mean."

Lina shifted uncomfortably. "We've grown very close."

"Oh, I know." Alex chuckled. "Lina this and Lina that. It's all I hear."

"He just appreciates the attention."

"It's not just him." Alex lowered her paper. "It's Claire and Nathan too. You walk on water around my house."

Your house, Lina thought. "Well, perhaps they appreciate the attention too."

"A regular do-gooder, are you?"

"I happen to like . . . *your* family."

"Oh yeah. They're a prize."

68

"You don't give them a chance."

"Hey, you know, living in my room for nine months doesn't make you an expert on my family." Alex lifted the paper back in front of her face, and Lina noticed for the first time that the print was Russian.

"You just buy that for the pictures, right?" She tried to lighten things up. No response. "You read Russian?"

"Uh-huh," Alex grunted.

"Alex . . ."

"Yeah?"

"I'm sorry if I offended you."

Alex peeked around the paper. "No problem. Forget about it." She tossed the paper aside. "Have you heard the joke about the three guys and the hooker?"

"Which one?"

"There's a hooker who lives on top of a mountain. One guy's climbing up to see her, one's in there with her, the third's on his way back down."

"So what's the joke?"

"It's more like a riddle. You have to guess their nationalities."

"Based on what?"

"It's not a left brain thing."

"Then I don't stand a chance."

"Just think about it." Lina pretended to ponder, and watched the blowing leaves cast shadows across Alex's legs.

"Got it?" Lina shook her head no. "OK. The guy on the way up is Russian. The one on the way down is Finnish. And the one inside with the hooker, Himalayan!"

Lina smiled. "Where did you learn Russian?"

"St. Petersburg. Or, I should say, Leningrad stumbling around in its new-world-order baby shoes."

"Nice metaphor."

"Heard it on CNN."

Lina buried her surprise under a casual "Hmm." Maybe there was more to Alex than met the eye — although what met the eye was plenty. "So, how did you end up there. I mean, why?"

"Why not? Sweet sixteen, I got to pick a place to go. I picked there."

"Interesting choice."

"Life shouldn't be boring."

"No, I guess not. But why Russia?"

"At first just to get back at Claire. But I ended up really liking it. They drink vodka like water!"

"Get back at Claire for what?"

"Oh, her little 'Russian phase'. The Dr. Zhivago video she watched endlessly in her bedroom . . . the parties she threw to parade Russian faculty members around on her arm . . . you know how she is."

Lina did know how she was. "That must've been something. How old were you?"

"Egg had just been introduced to sperm."

"She was pregnant?"

"Unexpectedly."

"So your real father worked at the university too?"

"My *only* father. He was a professor. Taught botany." Alex dug her smokes from her shirt pocket. "But then Claire upgraded to an administrator."

"Nathan . . ."

"Right-O!" She lit her cigarette.

"Then this Russian phase . . . it was before you were born?"

"And after, for a while."

"Seems like a long time to carry a grudge."

"Maybe. But its effects have stayed with me to this day."

"I understand." This was a picture Lina could paint from memory. "It's difficult to have a mother who's absent, regardless of whether the absence is physical or emotional. Freud said that multiple symptoms can be expected to . . ."

"Whoa-whoa-whoa." Alex waved her hand. "Slow down. It's way simpler than that. It's just the video."

"I don't understand."

Alex extended her hand. "Alexandra Zhivago Wilder, at your service."

Lina playfully pushed back Alex's hand. "You're joking."

"You're right." Alex grinned. "I'm not at anyone's service!"

For a second, Lina found Alex almost charming. "It could've been worse. She could've been watching *Battleship Potemkin*."

"I never thought about it like that."

"Battleship Potemkin Wilder!"

"OK, OK. Ixnay on the teasing."

"A sensitive streak?"

"Don't spread it around."

"Who would believe me?"

Alex smiled. "Oh, you're very believable. Must be the big, dark eyes or something. Bet they get you out of lots of trouble."

"And into it." Lina put on her most coquettish look. "Difficult to imagine, I know."

Alex puffed her cigarette. "Not *so* difficult..." She exhaled slowly.

"What's not so difficult?" Sean sat up, rubbing his eyes.

"I think we have company." Lina reached and rubbed his head, grateful for the interruption.

"I'm not sleepy." He yawned.

Lina checked her watch. "That was a very short nap."

"Let's go play Terminator!" He struggled to his feet. "The sleep fairy put quarters under my pillow!" He pulled a handful of change from his pocket.

"The sleep fairy?" Alex looked to Lina, who mouthed the word "Claire." "Hmm..." Alex looked back to Sean. "The sleep fairy never put quarters under my pillow!"

"They're for being good!" He grinned proudly.

"That explains it." Alex took a final puff of her smoke and mashed it out on her boot. She stood and brushed twigs from the backs of her legs. "So, let's go play Terminator. It's at Video Jones, right?"

"You've been?" Lina asked.

"I took her there." Sean pointed to himself.

"Yes you did." Alex lifted him into the air and bounced him. "And you kicked my butt! Didn't you?"

Sean giggled. "She said 'butt' again."

"That doesn't mean *you* can." Lina stood. "We have to clean up before we go anywhere." Alex put

Sean down, and Lina handed him a stack of paper plates and napkins. "These in there." She aimed him toward the recycling bin.

He waddled off obediently, mumbling "Butt-butt-butt-butt-butt-butt."

Alex laughed, and Lina glared at her. "Don't encourage him."

"Why not? He's just a kid."

"Exactly. And he'll pay for it after you leave."

"You mean he'll pay for it after *you* leave."

"Don't put that responsibility on me."

"I didn't."

Lina threw the last few items into the cooler and snapped it closed. "I'm driving." She lifted it and headed down the hill.

"There's a spot." Alex pointed as they made the turn onto Broadway. "Right in front of that psychic place."

Lina glanced at the flashing sign — "Madam Kalderas — Palms and Cards Read." She kept driving. "I'll find something closer."

"Are you crazy? The arcade's right across the street. And it's a miracle we even found a spot at this hour."

"Alright, fine." Lina put on her flasher and backed into the spot.

"We could go in and get a reading. It's been a long time, for me."

"What about Stargazer?"

"You remembered . . ." Alex smiled. "I don't have

the patience to wait. There's always too many people ahead of me. I liked talking to the people in the rooms though."

"Terminator!" Sean yelled from the back seat, recognizing where they were.

"You've got it, honey." Lina turned off the car and got out. She crossed to the passenger side and leaned into the back to unstrap Sean from his carseat. She could feel Alex's eyes on her from behind, and banged her head on the door frame as she lifted Sean out. "Merde!"

Alex smiled. "You know, just because you say it in French doesn't make it any different."

"Point taken." She put Sean down and took his hand.

"Terminator-Terminator-Terminator." He tugged her toward the crosswalk.

"Twenty-five dollars for a card reading," Alex called from behind them. "That's decent!"

"Twenty-five cents for a video game." Lina picked up speed. "You could play a hundred times. And know just as much about your future at the end."

Alex trotted to catch up with them. "You're a cynic."

"And you're naive."

"That's your cynicism speaking."

"This is an endless loop."

"Terminator!" Sean pulled free of Lina's hand and charged into the arcade. Lina chased after him, and Patsy Jones, sole proprietor of Video Jones, handed-off the green booster as she ran by.

"You were in here yesterday." Patsy nodded at Alex.

"Yes I was."

"You remember me?"

"Sorry. No."

"I remember you."

"Can I smoke in here?"

"Not supposed to, but I'll make an exception." Patsy pulled a Zippo from her pocket and offered Alex a light. "You asked that yesterday. I answered the same thing."

"Right, I remember now. Never mind though, I'll wait."

Patsy flipped the lighter shut and slid it back into her pocket. "You a friend of Lina's?"

"Sort of."

"She's a good woman."

"So I've heard."

"Comes in here two, three times a week with Sean. Usually sits starin' out the window while he burns through quarters. Patience of a saint, that woman. Don't think she's here cos she likes it or anything."

"I don't know. I've seen her play Nintendo with a vengeance."

"I try to make conversation with her, you know, to help pass the time. She found this place all the way from Greece. Did ya know that?"

"Huh?"

"On her computer. Said she was searching the area. I don't really get it. Too complicated. I'm a pinball kinda gal myself."

"I can see that." Alex pointed to the pinball machine tattooed on Patsy's forearm.

"My girlfriend did that. She works down the street at Skin Design."

"No way. What's her name?"

"Tempest."

Alex turned and pulled her T-shirt down off her shoulder. "Your girlfriend did this too!" Patsy admired the tiny angel perched on Alex's shoulder blade. "And this." Alex exposed her other shoulder, revealing the partner devil.

"Ingenious!" Patsy applauded.

"Tell her they've served me well."

"But it's us who serves them." She winked.

"You may be right." Alex fixed her shirt. "But I hope you're wrong."

"You're a smart one, aren't you?"

"Don't spread it around."

"I got news for you. It's obvious."

"Yeah, well, I think I'll test my brains at Tetris for awhile."

"Middle aisle, near the back, on the left." Patsy ejected a quarter from her change belt. "First game's on the house."

"Thanks." Alex headed off into the jungle of light and sound.

7

Sean was finally tucked in and sleeping, and Lina was ready for bed. It was only just past nine-thirty, but she'd been running on fumes for hours. She ran a hot bath and soaked for awhile, remembering different parts of the day. She wondered if Alex would be online tonight, and swore to herself she wouldn't go on.

But of course she did. Alex too had bathed, and was propped on her bed in her robe, laptop on her thighs. Lina had turned out all the lights, and was curled against the bay windows. The glow from her computer screen washed an eerie bluish-purple over her hands, as she typed in NXTDOOR and watched the hourglass flash.

YOU HAVE MAIL

Lina panicked. Nobody knew her under this screen name. Who could've sent mail to this account? She clicked the MAILBOX icon and tugged at her hair as a picture began to download onto her screen. Hair . . . dark and wavy. Blue eyes. Crimson lips. And then shoulders . . . bare, beautifully sculpted breasts . . . belly . . . legs for days . . .

HERE'S ME, AS PROMISED. PLAYGRL.

Lina smiled, mostly from relief, then hit DELETE. No sense accumulating evidence. She preferred to travel light.
She clicked the KEYWORD icon and typed in CRYSTAL BALL.

WELCOME TO THE CRYSTAL BALL FORUM.

She looked out across the pool. "Allright, Alexandra Zhivago Wilder. Where are you?"

ARCTICBLU: OBSERVER AND OBSERVED ARE
    INTIMATELY LINKED. ABSOLUTELY CANNOT
    BE SEPARATED.
NITECRONE: QUANTUM PHYSICS.
QUICKSAND: COMMON SENSE.
SHOCKRA: NOT EVERYONE WOULD AGREE.

QUICKSAND: THAT'S COS THEY'RE EGO-INVESTED.

NITECRONE: HEARD IT PAYS GOOD DIVIDENDS!

QUICKSAND: PRICE/EARNINGS RATIO IS TOO
    HIGH THO!

NITECRONE: WELCOME BACK, NXTDOOR.

NXTDOOR: HELLO.

NITECRONE: FIND STARGAZER LAST NIGHT?

NXTDOOR: I DID.

SHOCKRA: <--- GOT A READING FROM STARGAZER
    ONCE!

NXTDOOR: SEEMS LIKE EVERYONE HAS. EXCEPT
    ME.

NITECRONE: 2 LONG A WAIT?

NXTDOOR: THINK I WAS IN QUEUE, BUT DIDN'T
    STAY AROUND.

ARCTICBLU: WUNDRWMN IS IN THERE NOW. NEW
    ONLINE, BUT VERY INTUITIVE.

NITECRONE: SHE'S GOT LESS OF A FOLLOWING.
    MIGHT BE QUICKER.

KIZMET: TIME IS AN ARTIFACT!

NITECRONE: WELCOME BACK, KIZ.

Lina didn't want to sit through the time debate
again. She was already pretty certain Alex wasn't in
the room.

NXTDOOR: <--- GOING IN SEARCH OF WUNDRWMN.

KIZMET: AREN'T WE ALL! :-)

NITECRONE: SAFE TRAVELS, NXTDOOR.

NXTDOOR: THANK YOU. GOODNIGHT ALL.

Alex had flipped onto her stomach, bare legs
swinging in the air. Lina clicked the KEYWORD icon
and typed in NAKED TAROT. "Come to me, woman."

WELCOME TO NAKED TAROT
MERMADE: SO IS IT POSSIBLE I KNEW MY CAT
    IN A PAST LIFE?
WUNDERWMN: IT IS PROBABLE.
RUSHIN: SOULS ARE LIKE MAGNETS. THEY
    ATTRACT EACH OTHER, THEN STICK
    TOGETHER.
WUNDERWMN: WELL SAID.
RUSHIN: HEARD IT ON PBS! :-)

"Mon Dieu . . ." Lina pulled her fingers back from
the keyboard.

RUSHIN: HEY NXTDOOR. REMEMBER ME FROM
    LAST NIGHT?
NXTDOOR: OF COURSE.

Lina lied. But the name . . . it wouldn't have made
sense last night, wouldn't have caught her attention.

MERMADE: U 2 KNOW EACH OTHER?
RUSHIN: NOT EXACTLY. MET IN CRYSTAL BALL
    AND CAME IN HERE LOOKING FOR
    STARGAZER. SOMEONE ELSE WAS WITH
    HIM . . . WHAT WAS HER NAME?
NXTDOOR: DON'T REMEMBER.
WUNDRWMN: U HERE 4 A READING?
NXTDOOR: THOUGHT I'D JUST LISTEN IN FOR
    AWHILE.
WUNDRWMN: THAT'S FINE. WE'RE DISCUSSING
    PAST LIVES.

More concerned with her present life, Lina clicked on READ PROFILE and typed in RUSHIN.

SCREEN NAME: RUSHIN
FULL NAME: AS IF . . .
LOCATION: THIRD PLANET, NEAR THE WATER
BIRTH DATE: ARIES
MARITAL STATUS: NO
COMPUTER: ON MY LAP & HAPPY 2 B THERE
OCCUPATION: PRE-EMPLOYED
HOBBIES: HOWLING AT THE MOON ON RAINY
   NIGHTS
PERSONAL QUOTE: SYNCHRONICITY IS CHANCE . . .
   PERUSED, PURSUED, AND PERSUADED.

Entertaining, but devoid of clues. Perhaps that was the intention. Lina knew that game, and preferred to be on the other end of it. She tried to think up a quick I.M. to send RUSHIN — something friendly, not too forward, innocent sounding. But her scheming was cut short when her screen lit with an incoming message.

RUSHIN: R U THERE?

The hunter had been captured by the game . . .

NXTDOOR: <---
RUSHIN: U DITCHED OUT OF THE ROOM LAST
   NIGHT.

Lina stood and paced in a quick circle, trying to

shake off her nervous energy. It *had* to be Alex, if only because she so much wanted it to be. And that meant she had to compose both herself and a coherent reply.

NXTDOOR: LOW TOLERANCE FOR WAITING. DID YOU GET YOUR READING?

RUSHIN: NOT EXACTLY.

NXTDOOR: ?

RUSHIN: LOW TOLERANCE 4 WAITING TOO! IN QUEUE AGAIN NOW. FIFTEEN MINUTES ALREADY. THEY'LL I.M.

NXTDOOR: THAT WON'T DISCONNECT US?

RUSHIN: U CAN GET LOTS AT ONCE. HAVE DIFFERENT CONVERSATIONS GOING ON. ALL PRIVATE.

NXTDOOR: YOU KNOW A LOT ABOUT WCL.

RUSHIN: WCL???

NXTDOOR: WORLD COMPULINE.

RUSHIN: NO. JUST LEARNING. A FRIEND IS HELPING ME.

NXTDOOR: LIKE IT?

RUSHIN: SURE. LIKE TO EXPLORE. NEVER BEEN ANYWHERE LIKE THIS BEFORE.

NXTDOOR: THE NEW FINAL FRONTIER.

RUSHIN: JUST GOES TO SHOW U, THERE'S ALWAYS A FRONTIER PAST THE ONE YOU'RE AT NOW.

NXTDOOR: PHILOSOPHIC ...

RUSHIN: HAZARD OF BEING HUMAN!

NXTDOOR: AND WISE BEYOND YOUR YEARS.

RUSHIN: U KNOW MY AGE?

"Merde!" Lina glanced across at Alex, who leaned to light her cigarette on a candle.

NXTDOOR: THOUGHT YOU MENTIONED IT IN THE
    ROOM LAST NIGHT? EARLY 20'S?
RUSHIN: USUALLY SAY I'M "AGELESS" WHEN
    ASKED.
NXTDOOR: MUST BE THINKING OF SOMEONE
    ELSE.

Several moments passed without response, and Lina was sure she'd blown her cover.

RUSHIN: JUST GOT AN I.M. FROM WUNDRWMN.
    I'M UP NEXT. FINALLY!
NXTDOOR: I DO READINGS ALSO.

Lina typed the words without thinking.

RUSHIN: U DO?
NXTDOOR: YES. I COULD DO YOURS NOW, IF YOU
    WANT.
RUSHIN: WHAT DECK DO YOU USE?

Lina knew she was in over her head, but struggled to stay afloat.

NXTDOOR: COLLECTED CARDS THROUGH THE
    YEARS FROM DIFFERENT DECKS. MADE ONE
    COMPLETE DECK FROM THEM.
RUSHIN: I'VE NEVER HEARD OF THAT BEFORE.
NXTDOOR: <--- MARCH TO THE BEAT OF MY OWN
    DRUM.

RUSHIN: I LIKE THAT.

Score . . .

RUSHIN: OK, HANG ON. I'LL I.M. WUNDRWMN
    AND CANCEL.
NXTDOOR: I'LL GET MY CARDS.

Lina knew the true challenge was about to
begin — that fine balance between vagueness and
detail that would keep her anonymous, keep RUSHIN
hooked, and determine for sure if she had Alex on
the line.

RUSHIN: I'M BACK.
NXTDOOR: AT YOUR SERVICE.
RUSHIN: COOL TO FIND A GUY INTO THE CARDS.
    MOST I KNOW THINK IT'S HOCUS-POCUS. OR
    A COP-OUT.
NXTDOOR: GETS ME LOTS OF WOMEN.
RUSHIN: REALLY???

Apparently the subtleties of sarcasm did not travel
well in this venue.

NXTDOOR: NO. NOT REALLY. SO, DO YOU HAVE A
    SPECIFIC QUESTION?
RUSHIN: HOW COME U HAVE NO PROFILE?
NXTDOOR: I MEANT FOR YOUR READING.
RUSHIN: I KNOW. BUT HOW COME ANYWAY?
NXTDOOR: HAVEN'T GOTTEN AROUND TO IT YET.
RUSHIN: WHERE DO U LIVE?
NXTDOOR: MOVE AROUND A LOT.
RUSHIN: WHERE R U NOW?

NXTDOOR: WEST COAST.

RUSHIN: WHY SO MYSTERIOUS?

NXTDOOR: MYSTERIOUS??? WHAT ABOUT "THIRD PLANET, NEAR THE WATER?"

RUSHIN: A GIRL'S GOTTA HAVE HER SECRETS...

NXTDOOR: AGREED. SO, DO YOU HAVE A QUESTION OR TOPIC?

RUSHIN: EVERYTHING'S A QUESTION! U JUST DO A SPREAD AND TELL ME WHAT IT SAYS.

NXTDOOR: ARMOR.

RUSHIN: WHAT CARD IS THAT?

NXTDOOR: IT'S NOT A SPECIFIC CARD.

RUSHIN: ???

NXTDOOR: MY STYLE IS MORE OF AN INTUITIVE SYNTHESIS.

That sounded preposterous even to Lina.

RUSHIN: DON'T KNOW IF I'M BEING ADVENTUROUS OR NAIVE, BUT I'LL GIVE IT A SHOT.

NXTDOOR: YOU CARRY AN ARMOR OVER YOU. YOU THINK IT PROTECTS YOU.

RUSHIN: ARMOR DOES HAVE THAT EFFECT...

NXTDOOR: IT ONLY CUTS YOU OFF, OBSCURES YOUR TRUE NATURE. AND YOU KNOW THAT.

RUSHIN: YEAH, WELL EVERYTHING'S A TRADE OFF.

NXTDOOR: THERE'S ALSO FIRE AROUND YOU.

RUSHIN: MY CARDINAL ELEMENT.

NXTDOOR: ENERGY, ACTION, LIBIDO.

RUSHIN: A TRIPLE HEADER!

NXTDOOR: YOU HAVE POWER AT YOUR DISPOSAL.

RUSHIN: COOL!

NXTDOOR: BUT NOT YET UNDER YOUR CONTROL.
RUSHIN: <--- ALWAYS FORGETS TO READ THE
    FINE PRINT. SO, WHAT'S THE PROGNOSIS?
NXTDOOR: SOMEONE IN YOUR LIFE LOOKS UP
    TO YOU.
RUSHIN: WHO?
NXTDOOR: I WAS GOING TO ASK YOU THAT.
RUSHIN: NOBODY COMES TO MIND . . . EXCEPT MY
    BROTHER, BUT HE'S GOTTA LOOK UP TO ME
    COS HE'S ABOUT 3 FEET TALL!

"Alex . . ."

NXTDOOR: BE MORE AWARE OF THAT POSITION.
RUSHIN: IS THAT U TALKING OR THE CARDS?
NXTDOOR: WOULD EITHER MAKE IT LESS TRUE?
RUSHIN: NEVER BEEN AFRAID OF TRUTH. IT
    SOMETIMES HURTS THE EGO, BUT ALWAYS
    HEALS THE SOUL.
NXTDOOR: I LIKE THAT.
RUSHIN: GOT IT FROM A BUDDHISM SEMINAR.
NXTDOOR: WHAT'S YOUR INTERPRETATION?
RUSHIN: WHEN SHITTY THINGS HAPPEN, THROW
    A PARTY. HEY, HANG ON A MINUTE . . .
NXTDOOR: WHAT DO U MEAN?

Lina waited, but there was no response. She
looked across the pool. Alex was gone, but quickly
reappeared carrying Sean piggy-back. She plopped him
down on the bed and sat beside him. He pointed to
her laptop, and she placed it between them.

RUSHIN: SORRY. JUST GOT COMPANY.
NXTDOOR: AT THIS HOUR?

RUSHIN: CAN'T SEEM TO KEEP THE MEN AWAY!!!
NXTDOOR: ARE YOU TRYING TO MAKE ME
    JEALOUS? :-)
RUSHIN: R U SAYING I COULD IF I TRIED???
NXTDOOR: <--- NOT THE JEALOUS TYPE.
RUSHIN: OF COURSE NOT. RWE930009J3NCKL
    SIS00'[0WI3 \'LS K[PW]]P=]E\PPWJJOV
NXTDOOR: MATH EQUATION?
RUSHIN: LOL! SORRY! MY VISITOR LIKES TO GET
    HIS HANDS INTO THINGS.
NXTDOOR: SHALL WE TALK ANOTHER TIME?
RUSHIN: I'LL LOOK 4 U. I'M USUALLY ON AT
    NIGHT.
NXTDOOR: I AM TOO. ENJOY.
RUSHIN: THANX. BYE.
NXTDOOR: GOODNIGHT.

Alex slung Sean over her shoulder and carried him out of the room. She returned several minutes later, dropped her robe to the floor, and slid into bed. The candle went out with a puff. That was the last thing Lina remembered.

8

A TOWERING TREE WITH TANGLED BRANCHES
WRAPS AROUND ITSELF, UMBILICAL-LIKE, UNTIL
IT STRANGLES, SUFFOCATES AND TURNS INTO A
PILLAR OF STONE. SILVER SWORDS OF
THUNDERBOLT SLASH THE FACES OF DARK
PLANETS THAT LOOK LIKE EYES AND OOZE
BLOOD THAT IS THICKER THAN WATER. DOUBLE
STRANDS COIL AND SINK INTO BLACKER THAN
BLACK MIDNIGHT CATACOMBS THAT SWALLOW
THE BREATH OF THE WIND, LEAVING LESS
THAN NOTHING.

Lina sprung awake, gasping for breath, and tumbled to the floor. Her dark, disheveled hair stuck out in all directions, and her black eyes flashed wildly back and forth, desperate to lock on solid surroundings. A tree branch tapped against the windowpane . . . the sky was seven shades of gray . . . the pool water, pocked with tiny splashes. It was pouring rain, and it was 8:37 a.m.

She pulled herself up into the recessed seating where, apparently, she'd spent the night. She discovered the ache of her elbows and knees as she dressed and made a dash for the main house. The sting of rain felt good against her face, and she let the wind carry her toward the door.

She took the stairs three at a time, relieved to find Sean sleeping safely in his bed. "Honey." She rubbed his back gently. He rolled over and looked up at her, bleary-eyed.

"You're wet."

"It's raining outside."

"We could put on galoshes and go run in it." He sat up and swung his legs off the bed. Lina noticed he was in his underwear again, but couldn't afford the sidetrack.

"You have Play-Care today, remember?"

"Raptors and Tyrannosaurus Rex! We get to cut them out and paste them on Miss Betty's walls."

"Well, listen. I slept later than I was supposed to, so we have to hurry to get there on time. OK?" Not to mention that she was due in Cognitive Psych lab at nine.

"White today!" He pointed to her blouse.

"Right, fine." She pulled a white polo from his closet. "How about this one?"

"Yes, please." He reached for it and pulled it over his head.

"You slept late today too." Lina handed him a pair of khaki shorts and underwear.

"I visited Alex last night!"

"Really?"

He nodded vigorously. "I woke up and I went to Mom's door, but then I didn't go in. And then music was downstairs, so I went down there to go see Alex."

"And then?" She quickly made up his bed.

"I typed on her computer, and then she told me a story." He put a finger to his lips, thinking. "And then I went to bed, and then you woke me up." He stepped into his shorts and pulled them up. "Zip."

Lina smiled. "You zip. I'm going down to the kitchen to pour you some cereal. You can eat it in the car."

"Is Alex coming with us?"

"Not today." She wagged a finger at his shorts. "Zip-zip-zip."

Cognitive Psych class was a blur, except that Pam, the Teacher's Assistant, had on the most extraordinary perfume. Lina caught its scent each time Pam paced the aisle, which she did continuously as she spoke. She started a little fantasy with Pam in it, but cut it short when her eyes drifted to the clock and saw it was only 10 a.m. Way too early for that sort of thing, and school was not the appropriate place.

The noon bell rang before the sign-up sheet got

passed to her, and Lina debated whether to stay and commit herself to a month of assisting Pam with her dissertation research. It was only worth half a credit, but it would mean three evenings a week tucked away in an office with Pam. And then she began to think of all the potential disappointments and complications, and she grabbed her book bag and made her escape.

"Hold my hand, OK?" Lina unstrapped Sean from his carseat and flipped up the hood of his raincoat in preparation for the sprint to the house. "It's slippery."

"I like it." Sean grinned and slid out of the car. Lina held the umbrella over him.

"Hey you guys . . ." Alex's voice came from the patio. "Over here."

Sean took off through the garden along the trail blazed by the Miata. Lina chased behind, sliding through the mud in her new loafers.

"You guys should come in." Alex was floating mid-pool, buoyed by a beach ball. "The water's really warm and the rain's really cold. It feels amazing."

"Let's go get my bathing suit!" Sean yanked Lina's raincoat.

"You must be crazy." She pulled him under the umbrella.

"Crazy is right!" Alex tossed the ball at Sean. "Just drop your clothes, little boy, and come on in."

Sean looked to Lina for permission. "Forget about it." She took him by the hand. "Your mother would have a coronary."

"She's not that uptight." Alex swam to the steps and sat down. "Besides, I'll be responsible."

Right, Lina thought, and I'll be asked to have a talk with you about it later. She bent to Sean's eye level. "How about a game of Nintendo instead?" He shook his head and turned to Alex for backup.

"She's the boss." Alex shrugged.

The comment surprised Lina, who suddenly didn't feel like the boss at all. Instead she felt uncomfortable, slightly buzzed and unnerved by the sight of Alex staring up at her with rain dripping down her face. "Let's go, Sean."

"You could come play Nintendo with us," he offered. "We could do a three-way game."

"I'll be in after a bit." Alex pulled her hair back and twisted the water from it. "You go on ahead."

"Come on, then." Lina tugged Sean toward the house.

"Hey," Alex called after them. "I got a phenomenal reading online last night. It would've made a believer out of even you."

Lina stopped and turned. "I doubt that."

"Well, it's true."

"I would bet . . ." Lina paused to choose her words, "that it was entirely vague." She walked backwards toward the house as she spoke. "Mostly fishing for information. Probably could've applied to me as much as to you."

Alex considered this. "That last part may just be true." She smiled. "But the rest of it's totally wrong. You can't fake something like that."

Lina opened the French doors and nudged Sean into the den. She wished she could play her trump card, but she also felt a pang of guilt about the ruse.

If she'd been the superstitious type, she might have wondered if her nightmares had returned as some sort of cosmic payback for her deception. But luckily, she was far too logical to fret over such a possibility. At least for more than a week or two.

9

After that first three-way Nintendo game, late-afternoon grudge matches had become a ritual. Sean was squaring off against Alex when Claire discreetly signaled to Lina from the hall. Lina excused herself, unnoticed.

"You are working wonders, my dear," Claire said when they were out of earshot. "It's almost just like a family." She turned Lina to face the den.

"I can't take credit for that."

"It's a very strange thing." Claire lowered her voice. "Just between you and me, I think she's trying to impress you. I don't remember ever seeing her so . . . agreeable."

Lina tugged nervously at her hair. The last thing she wanted was praise for arousing any interest on Alex's part. "I think Sean brings that out in her."

"Oh no, she's never been fond of him. Not that I don't understand, mind you. Sibling rivalry and blended families . . . I've seen it all on Sally Jessy."

"But I thought, I mean, Sean told me that Alex left before he was born."

"She left *because* he was born, dear."

A shriek came from the den. "AHHH! You killed me!" Alex rolled onto the floor and Sean jumped on top of her.

"Mommmmm! I killed her!" He pinned Alex down.

Claire stepped tentatively into the room. "That's wonderful, darling." She adjusted her mother of pearl barrette.

"Great hair clip." Alex flipped Sean off of her and struggled to her feet. "It's you against him now." She nodded to Lina. "I'm off to work on my archeology paper." She winked.

"Don't overdo it," Lina whispered as Alex passed on her way out.

"I stopped at the wharf." Nathan strode into the kitchen and swung five large bags onto the counter. "Compliments of Pike Place Market."

Lina pulled her head out of the fridge. "Welcome home."

"We have scallions, potatoes, broccoli and basmati." He presented the items like game show prizes. "We have tomatoes, capers and corn on the cob, feta cheese, and some boursin for good measure. We have garlic and gnocchi and sourdough and watermelon. We even have Greek olives, in your honor." He chuckled.

"Well, that solves that problem." Lina swung the fridge door shut.

"And this baby here was swimming an hour ago." He tossed a huge salmon onto the counter. Lina cringed, preferring to think of salmon as filleted, grilled, and buttered. "Don't worry." He pulled off his cufflinks and dropped them into his shirt pocket. "I'll cook it up." He rolled up his sleeves.

Lina could remember him cooking only twice before — Sean's birthday barbecue, and his own five-year anniversary with Claire. Both had been impressive spreads.

"I like being in the kitchen." He pulled a large pan from the hanging rack. "Something about all the smells, the commotion. I cooked a lot in my younger days."

"You don't really expect us to believe you were ever young, do you?" Alex swung into the kitchen and held out a stack of papers. "It's just a first draft and it's not finished yet, but I thought maybe you could look over it and, you know, tell me what you think."

"I'd be happy to." Nathan took the papers and glanced at Lina with a look that clearly gave her all the credit. Alex caught the look too, which made Lina feel even worse. She knew she should speak up, but she also knew she could count on Alex to make the point herself.

"Just so you know . . ." Alex elbowed Nathan and

dug her smokes from her pocket. "I was just kidding before. About you being young, I mean." Nathan fixed his eyes on the cigarettes. "Want one?" She snickered. "Kidding again. I know. I'm on my way out. I'll be down by the water if anyone needs me." She headed for the side door, then spied the loaf of sourdough. "Hey, can I have a mouthful of that to tide me over?"

"Help yourself." Nathan reached for a bread knife as Alex ripped into the loaf.

"This too?" She held up the boursin.

"With a knife." He handed it to her, and she spread some cheese across the slab of bread.

"For you." She held it out to him.

"Don't mind if I do." He cupped his hand to catch the crumbs.

"And you." She offered one to Lina — who, shocked by the whole interaction, eyed her with suspicion. "It's not poison." Alex took a bite, then held it up to Lina's mouth. "Promise."

Lina leaned forward and nibbled the crust. "Thank you."

"You didn't get any cheese." Alex rotated the bread and touched it to Lina's lips. "Here, try again."

Lina bit into a small piece which ripped fully across and dangled from her mouth. She tried to gracefully chew and swallow it, all the while watching Nathan from the corner of her eye. She wondered what he must be thinking . . . but then again, what was there to think? It was *she* who was thinking things. Things that would be better left unthought.

Alex stuffed her mouth with the remaining bread. "Ah cun muk a minsaz fur thasaman ef yawan." She signaled that she needed to finish chewing. "I said," she swallowed, "I can make a mean sauce for that salmon if you want."

Nathan tried to conceal his surprise. "I'd like that very much." He nodded.

"Back in a flash then." Alex slipped out the side door and headed down toward the dock.

"Remind me to give you a raise." Nathan unhooked the cutting board from the rack.

"Sir?"

"This is working out even better than I'd hoped." He pulled a knife from the drawer.

Lina was feeling worse by the second. "I had nothing to do with her writing that paper."

"Of course you did." He began filleting the salmon. "Maybe you didn't tell her what to write, maybe you didn't tell her anything at all. But your presence here is most certainly responsible for the change in her behavior. And I, for one, want to thank you. Whatever it is you're doing, keep it up." He gave her an awkward thumbs up.

"Yes, do keep it up, darling." Claire stepped in from the hall and added her own thumbs up.

Lina felt like she was in a strange dream or maybe a Fellini movie. "Right . . ."

"Hors d'oeuvre?" Nathan sliced a wedge of boursin onto a piece of sourdough, then topped it with an olive and offered it to Claire.

"Oh, I shouldn't. It'll spoi . . ." Nathan pushed it gently into her mouth. Claire looked shocked, then amused, then almost sad.

"You haven't fed me since our wedding."

"Shame on me." Nathan sliced a piece of feta and dropped a caper on top.

"I'll be upstairs with Sean." Lina backed toward the hall. "Just give a shout when you need help with the cooking."

"Will do." Nathan winked.

Nathan never did call for help, but he did outdo himself with the meal. Alex never once mentioned being vegetarian as she devoured her salmon. And Sean invented the game of spitting watermelon seeds into a bowl across the table, which Claire tolerated if not condoned.

After dinner, Lina said her goodnights and excused herself for the evening. She ran a scalding bath and sprinkled in some marine salts, which Alex swore by and had insisted she try. The familiar scent quickly mixed with steam and filled the room — and as Lina sank into the water, she could feel Alex's presence all around her.

She had herself wrapped in a towel and planted by the window at 11:47 p.m. The plan was that Alex would look for her, or rather, for Zack, around midnight. The nook was already set — laptop open and booted up, metaphysics books stacked by the window for quick reference, legal pads scribbled with the details of "Topics Discussed" and "Facts About Zack."

This would be their sixth visit online in the past twenty-two days, and Lina found that her navigation between the two worlds was demanding increasing vigilance. On the veranda tonight, under a full, yellow moon, someone had almost tried to kiss Alex goodnight. Lina wasn't sure if it was her or Zack.

RUSHIN: R U THERE?

She reached and switched off the light.

NXTDOOR: <---
RUSHIN: HEY ZACK! THE MOST AMAZING BALL
    OF GOLD IS HOVERING JUST OUTSIDE MY
    WINDOW.
NXTDOOR: AN ANGEL, PERHAPS?
RUSHIN: NO DOUBT. HOW R U?
NXTDOOR: BATHED AND SHAVED.
RUSHIN: GOING SOMEWHERE?
NXTDOOR: BIG DATE WITH MY PILLOW.
RUSHIN: HOW COME U NEVER MENTION
    WOMEN . . .
NXTDOOR: WHAT ABOUT THEM?
RUSHIN: NO PLAYING DUMB.
NXTDOOR: NONE WORTH MENTIONING.
RUSHIN: SOME WORTH NOT MENTIONING?
NXTDOOR: SOME.
RUSHIN: I WAS THINKING ABOUT U EARLIER
    TONITE.
NXTDOOR: THINKING WHAT?
RUSHIN: DIFFERENT THINGS. THINGS I'VE
    THOUGHT BEFORE.
NXTDOOR: SUCH AS?
RUSHIN: SUCH AS WHAT U LOOK LIKE, HOW U
    DRESS, DO U HAVE A NICE SMILE?

NXTDOOR: :-) <--- WHAT DO YOU THINK?
RUSHIN: LOL! IT'S CHARMING.
NXTDOOR: CYBERSPACE — THE GREAT EQUALIZER.
RUSHIN: U KNOW WHAT A GIF IS?
NXTDOOR: YES.
RUSHIN: HAVE ONE?
NXTDOOR: YES.
RUSHIN: WHY HAVEN'T I SEEN IT?
NXTDOOR: YOU HAVEN'T ASKED.
RUSHIN: BEEN SENT TONS I DIDN'T ASK FOR.
NXTDOOR: THAT'S NOT MY STYLE.
RUSHIN: I KNOW. THAT'S WHY I'M ASKING.
NXTDOOR: YOU ARE?
RUSHIN: I AM.
NXTDOOR: LATER, AFTER WE'RE FINISHED
    TALKING.
RUSHIN: COME ON . . .

Lina looked across the pool and tried to fight the feeling Alex was growing suspicious. She turned her screen even farther away from the window, obscuring its glow.

NXTDOOR: FINE, THEN. I'LL BE RIGHT BACK.

She clicked into her file directory and searched through the list of GIF's she'd downloaded during a recent venture online. Preparing for the eventuality of this request, she'd donned the screen name "PRNZCHRMNG," made just enough small talk to be noticed in the "CUTE BOYZ SEEK SAME" room, and accumulated eight GIF's in twenty minutes — unsolicited. She knew what Alex meant about that.

But which to choose? Five of them were nudes, and of the remaining three, "BOYWONDR" most resembled her. Dark hair, dark eyes, strong jawline, prominent lips. Hopefully the good looks would distract from the Harley . . .

She uploaded the GIF, changed the title to ZACK, and clicked SEND.

RUSHIN: U R A PRETTY BOY, AREN'T U?

NXTDOOR: THINK SO?

RUSHIN: U NEVER MENTIONED THE BIKE.

NXTDOOR: RECREATIONAL.

RUSHIN: RECREATING IS IMPORTANT! :-)

NXTDOOR: DO YOU RIDE?

RUSHIN: TRADED MY FIRST CAR 4 A BIKE IN
    BOARDING SCHOOL. BUMMED RIDES HOME
    FOR A YEAR. MY FOLKS WOULD'VE FREAKED,
    ACCUSED ME OF TRYING 2 MAKE A
    STATEMENT.

NXTDOOR: WERE YOU?

RUSHIN: I DON'T HAVE ANY GIF'S OF ME.

NXTDOOR: NICE SEGUE . . .

RUSHIN: U R NOT CURIOUS?

NXTDOOR: <--- VIVID IMAGINATION.

RUSHIN: U HAVE IMAGINED ME?

NXTDOOR: NOT INCESSANTLY . . . BUT YES.

RUSHIN: LIKE WHAT?

NXTDOOR: NOTHING SPECIFIC.

RUSHIN: TELL ME. IMAGINE NOW.

NXTDOOR: I IMAGINE WE'RE TOGETHER AT A
    SIDEWALK CAFE SOMEWHERE. NO COMPUTER
    BETWEEN US. ONLY ESPRESSO AND
    CHOCOLATES.

RUSHIN: GODIVA CHOCOLATES.

NXTDOOR: AND MAYBE STRAWBERRIES.

RUSHIN: STRAWBERRIES DON'T GO WITH
ESPRESSO.

NXTDOOR: RIGHT. MAKE IT CHAMPAGNE.

RUSHIN: IN TALL FROSTED GLASSES WITH
ORANGE TWISTS ON THE RIM.

NXTDOOR: SOMETHING BOLD BY VIVALDI
PLAYING IN THE BACKGROUND.

RUSHIN: FOUR SEASONS.

NXTDOOR: AUTUMN.

RUSHIN: AUTUMN: LA CACCIA.

NXTDOOR: YOU KNOW YOUR VIVALDI.

RUSHIN: DON'T TELL. WOULD TARNISH MY
REPUTATION!

NXTDOOR: WHICH ONE?

RUSHIN: THE FEMME FATALE ONE THAT SCARES
GUYS OFF.

NXTDOOR: VIVALDI MIGHT SCARE OFF MORE
THAN A FEW GUYS.

RUSHIN: BUT NOT U.

NXTDOOR: NO.

RUSHIN: WHAT SCARES U?

NXTDOOR: ANTHONY HOPKINS, SILENCE OF THE
LAMBS.

RUSHIN: NO, SERIOUSLY.

NXTDOOR: WOMEN ASKING QUESTIONS ABOUT
ME.

RUSHIN: WHY?

NXTDOOR: DON'T KNOW. MAYBE GYPSY BLOOD.

RUSHIN: A.K.A. FEAR OF INTIMACY.

NXTDOOR: PREFER TO THINK OF IT AS LOVE OF
FREEDOM.

RUSHIN: THUS THE HARLEY...

"Entirely fortuitous."

NXTDOOR: EXACTLY.
RUSHIN: I THINK IT'S FEAR.
NXTDOOR: OF WHAT?
RUSHIN: THE USUAL. ATTACHMENT, COMMIT-
    MENT, TAKING RISKS.
NXTDOOR: I'VE BEEN ATTACHED. IT WASN'T
    ESPECIALLY GRATIFYING.
RUSHIN: TO WHO?
NXTDOOR: A WOMAN. WHEN I WAS YOUNGER.
RUSHIN: AND?
NXTDOOR: GYPSY BLOOD.
RUSHIN: U DITCHED.
NXTDOOR: NO, SHE DID.
RUSHIN: AND TOOK YOUR HEART.
NXTDOOR: SOMETHING ALONG THOSE LINES.
RUSHIN: U GOTTA GET OVER THAT KINDA STUFF.
NXTDOOR: <--- WASN'T BORN WITH THE
    INSTRUCTIONS.
RUSHIN: NOBODY COMES WITH INSTRUCTIONS. U
    FIGURE IT OUT AS U GO ALONG. THAT'S THE
    WHOLE POINT.
NXTDOOR: OF WHAT?
RUSHIN: THE UNIVERSE.
NXTDOOR: DON'T GET GRANDIOSE ON ME.
RUSHIN: CHANGE AND EVOLUTION. THAT'S ALL
    THERE IS.
NXTDOOR: HOW DOES THAT FIT WITH
    ATTACHMENT AND COMMITMENT?
RUSHIN: HAVE 2 GET BACK 2 U ON THAT ONE.

NXTDOOR: WOULD SEEM TO MAKE MORE OF AN
ARGUMENT AGAINST IT.

RUSHIN: THE UNIVERSE IS ALSO BIG ON IRONY
AND PARADOX.

NXTDOOR: WE AGREE ON THAT.

RUSHIN: BUT THAT'S JUST IT. WHEN U R MOST
CONFUSED, THAT'S WHEN U HAVE 2 PAY
MOST ATTENTION. SOMETHING'S TRYING 2
IMPRESS ITSELF ON U.

NXTDOOR: DO YOU SIT AROUND AT NIGHT AND
THINK THESE THINGS UP?

RUSHIN: I TALK A GOOD GAME ... BUT ACTUALLY
I SIT AROUND AND TRY 2 FIGURE OUT HOW
2 PRACTICE WHAT I PREACH. :-) HOW DID WE
GET OFF ON THIS TANGENT ANYWAY?

NXTDOOR: ATTACHMENT, COMMITMENT, RISK
TAKING ...

RUSHIN: OH YEAH. TELL ME ABOUT THE WOMAN.

NXTDOOR: THE WOMAN?

RUSHIN: WHO DITCHED U.

NXTDOOR: NOT MUCH TO TELL.

RUSHIN: COME ON ...

NXTDOOR: WE WERE TOGETHER FOR FIVE
YEARS. AND THEN WE WEREN'T.

RUSHIN: 5 YEARS ... SOUNDS SERIOUS.

NXTDOOR: I THOUGHT SO.

RUSHIN: WHAT HAPPENED?

NXTDOOR: DON'T REALLY KNOW. HEARD SHE
NEEDED FREEDOM.

RUSHIN: HEARD FROM SOMEONE ELSE?

NXTDOOR: RELIABLE THIRD PARTY.

RUSHIN: SHE DIDN'T TELL U?

NXTDOOR: NOT A WORD.

RUSHIN: OUCH.

NXTDOOR: RIGHT.

RUSHIN: AND THEN WHAT?

NXTDOOR: THEN THOSE WOMEN NOT WORTH
MENTIONING.

RUSHIN: WHY NOT WORTH MENTIONING?

NXTDOOR: DIDN'T MAKE A BIG IMPRESSION.

RUSHIN: U OR THEM?

NXTDOOR: BOTH, I SUPPOSE. WHAT ABOUT YOU?

RUSHIN: WHAT ABOUT ME?

NXTDOOR: MEN?

RUSHIN: LOTS, OF COURSE.

NXTDOOR: ANYONE SPECIAL?

RUSHIN: JUST ONE.

Lina did a quick rundown of the possibilities.
There was Pete-Gepetto, and the boyfriend she'd
spent Christmas with instead of coming home, and
the guys from Montana. Nobody else came to mind,
but Alex *had* crossed through a lot of states.

NXTDOOR: HOW COME YOU NEVER MENTIONED
HIM?

RUSHIN: I HAVE.

NXTDOOR: YOUR BROTHER . . .

RUSHIN: THAT'S THE MOST I CARE 2 HANDLE BY
WAY OF RELATIONSHIPS RIGHT NOW! EXCEPT
FOR THIS ONE, OF COURSE.

NXTDOOR: THIS ONE?

RUSHIN: YEAH. US.

NXTDOOR: DOES THIS CONSTITUTE A
RELATIONSHIP?

RUSHIN: DON'T GET YOUR LITTLE INNER GYPSY
IN A PANIC. I MEANT . . . NOT A BIG "R"
RELATIONSHIP, JUST A LITTLE "R"
RELATIONSHIP.
NXTDOOR: AS IN, A LITTLE "F" FRIENDSHIP?
RUSHIN: MAYBE BIG "F" FRIENDSHIP. BUT NOT
TIME FOR A PRENUPTIAL OR ANYTHING. :-)
NXTDOOR: ONLY WANT WHAT I CAME IN WITH.
RUSHIN: FAIR ENOUGH. BUT IT NEVER REALLY
WORKS OUT THAT WAY, DOES IT?
NXTDOOR: IN WHAT SENSE?
RUSHIN: U ALWAYS LOSE SOMETHING. WHEN
SOMEONE WALKS, A PIECE OF U GOES.
NXTDOOR: SO THEN, YOU'RE LEFT WITH LESS
THAN WHAT YOU CAME IN WITH?
RUSHIN: LESS, AND MORE. BECAUSE NOW U
HAVE A PIECE OF THEM TOO.
NXTDOOR: SO EVENTUALLY YOU HAVE LOTS OF
PIECES OF OTHER PEOPLE AND NOTHING
LEFT OF YOURSELF.
RUSHIN: MAKE U WANNA HOP ON YOUR HARLEY?
NXTDOOR: TRADING IT IN FOR A CESSNA!
RUSHIN: LOL! HEY, I GOTTA GET SOME SHUT
EYE. WHEN CAN U TALK AGAIN?

Lina was in no mood to commit, big *or* little "C."

NXTDOOR: MAYBE I'LL SURPRISE YOU. ARE YOU
STILL ON MOST NIGHTS?
RUSHIN: U BET. PAST FEW NIGHTS I'VE LOGGED
INTO THE LIBRARY OF CONGRESS AND
DOWNLOADED INFO FOR A PAPER I'M

WORKING ON. BEATS THE HELL OUT OF
DEWEY DECIMAL.

NXTDOOR: THEN I'LL LOOK FOR YOU IN THE
STACKS.

RUSHIN: SOUNDS LIKE FUN.

NXTDOOR: GOODNIGHT.

RUSHIN: LATER.

10

"That looks exquisite!" The saleswoman paced in a half-circle behind Lina. "And you have the body for it too, God bless ya."

Lina stared at her three reflections in the mirrored alcove. The dress was simple, classic looking. Black with thin straps over the shoulder. "I like it very much." She turned and looked back at herself from behind.

"Of course, that black and white checkered skirt with the jacket looked gorgeous too." The woman primped her gray-blue hair. "Perhaps you'd like both.

One for tonight, one for the next special occasion."
She winked.

"Oh, no." Lina slid the straps off her shoulders.
"I couldn't afford them both. But I will take this
one." She stepped back into the dressing room.

"Just slip out of it and hand it over the door,
and I'll get you started at the register."

Lina reconsidered as she redressed. She checked
the tag again, as if somehow the price might have
gone down from $97 since she last looked. It seemed
an exorbitant amount, but Nathan had stuck an extra
$100 bill in with yesterday's paycheck, and she was
anxious to get rid of it. "A bonus for service above
and beyond," he'd jotted on the envelope. But she'd
felt embarrassed and guilty, and worried he was
getting more than he'd bargained for.

She tucked the shopping bag into her carrier and
decided to bike home the long way. She'd thought
Friday would never arrive, but now that it had, she
wished it were already over. It was getting hard to
even look at Alex without feeling like a liar and a
hypocrite — and the more she grew to respect her,
the less she respected herself. In a twisted way, it
had been easier to be attracted to someone she
loathed.

"Madam Kalderas." The sign flashed at Lina like
a taunt. She slowed her pace and glanced non-
chalantly in the storefront window. A young man sat
at the round table, an array of cards spread before
him against the black velvet cloth. Across from him
was a striking woman with wild, black hair and olive
skin. She glanced up at Lina and nodded.

"Fools." Lina pedaled away quickly. "The future

cannot be predicted," she assured herself. And to prove her point, she stopped on impulse and bought a pair of shoes on the next block, and a clutch purse on the block after that.

Lina was ready twenty minutes early, and sat on her bed waiting to hear Alex come out the front door. She composed the speech in her head, the confession where she would tell Alex everything and try to make light of it before it went too far. But she couldn't get past the feeling that it had already gone too far. Zack had been invented as a way of getting closer to Alex, but now he just seemed to be standing between them, assuring they'd never be close. Perhaps that was for the best.

"You dressed," Lina said dryly as she crossed the driveway toward Alex, who sat on the hood of her Miata.

"Long pants." Alex looked down at her new jeans and shiny black boots. "That's dressed!" She hopped down and unlocked the passenger door for Lina. "Got my car back, finally. They had to vacuum the motor or something, and replace a shitload of parts." Lina slid in silently and unlocked the other door. She tucked her purse under the seat as Alex climbed in and revved the engine. "Sounds great, doesn't it?"

"It's a marvel."

"Listen . . ." Alex rolled down her window and lit a smoke. "Don't take it personally, OK?"

"To what are you referring?"

Alex stretched an arm behind Lina's seat and

turned to back down the driveway. "I had to wear dresses every day for three years at St. Michael's. Not just dresses, these awful red and green plaid things that made you want to yodel or something. I just can't do it anymore. Unless a priest is gonna be there."

"Excuse me?"

"Weddings, funerals, you know. Places you have to wear a dress ... out of respect for God or something."

"You believe in God?"

"Sure." Alex sounded surprised. "Don't you?"

"Sure," Lina said. But she wasn't. She was only sure about things that were, well, sure. Like the fact that she was feeling exceptionally nervous and almost school-girlish racing down the expressway beside her boss's daughter. And that the scent of leather seats and the colored twinkle of dashboard lights were somehow making the whole thing feel suspiciously like a date.

"There she blows!" Alex pointed to the flashing lights as they pulled off of I-5. She made a quick turn into the huge parking lot and pulled up in front of the building. "Valet's only two bucks. It's worth it not to have to wander around in the dark after a few drinks, searching for your car like an idiot." She took the ticket from the doorman and pushed through the revolving door. Lina followed warily.

The room was massive, brightly lit and crowded with purposeful people moving quickly about. "They have bingo over there on Tuesdays." Alex pointed to a section that was cordoned off. "Never been, but I think it'd be fun." She took Lina by the hand and moved her through the crowd to a row of blackjack tables. "This is my territory!" she announced proudly, reminding Lina of Sean.

"Five dollar minimum," Lina read the small placard. "Where are the slot machines?"

"Don't have any in Washington. Not allowed. But cards are more fun anyway. You have more control."

"It's still a matter of luck. That's why it's called *gambling.*"

"But luck can be . . . summoned. Besides, you choose what to do with the hand you're dealt. That's where the real gamble is."

Lina sensed a message in that, which she chose to ignore. "I think I'll just watch."

"Oh, come on. Don't be a party-pooper." Alex swung her arm over Lina's shoulder. "Let's sit at that table." She pointed. "I have a good feeling about it."

Lina looked over at the table. It wasn't the only one with available seats, but it was the one with the handsomest dealer. "You mean you have a good feeling about *him.*"

"Doesn't hurt!" Alex winked. "Does he have the bluest eyes or what?" She hopped up on a stool and tapped the one next to her. Only the smallest tinge of jealousy ran through Lina, or was it Zack, before she reined it in and sat down. Alex dropped fifty dollars on the table and scooped up her stack of chips. "Here." She slid half the pile to Lina.

"Oh, no." Lina pushed it back. "But thanks. I have my own." She removed twenty dollars from her purse and handed it to the dealer.

After an hour of playing, Lina was fifteen dollars ahead of Alex. "Need a loan?" She nudged Alex with her elbow.

"Put your money where your mouth is." Alex knocked back her third Midori on the rocks.

"What do you mean by that?"

Alex glanced at the card deck, which was almost fully used and would soon be reshuffled. "Put it all down on the next hand and I'll do the same."

"You're crazy. Or intoxicated. I'll be driving home."

"It's gonna be a rich hand. I have a good feeling about it."

Lina balked, but Alex *had* won almost every hand she'd had a "good feeling" about. "I'll start with half."

"Do what you want." Alex smiled. "Like my dad used to say, you gotta trust your instincts." She pushed all of her chips in front of her and was dealt a five. "Of course, my instincts were wrong about him too." She shrugged.

Jesting aside, Lina realized this was the first time she'd heard Alex say anything about her feelings toward her father. The topic of his absence was off-limits — a stance which Lina could relate to and, as such, respected. Turning her attention back to the game, she tried not to look overly self-righteous when the dealer flipped an ace in front of her. She and Alex both watched silently as second cards were dealt around the table. Alex landed a ten. "Shit."

Lina drew a second ace and checked the dealer's hand. He had a three facing up. "You should stick." She motioned to Alex's cards. "Let the dealer bust. The odds are against him."

"Which means they're with us. And you should split those aces. Two hands, two chances to win."

"Or lose." Lina thumbed through her stack of chips. "I'd have to put all the rest of my money down."

"Right." Alex signaled for a third card and drew a six. "Yes!" She hopped down from her stool and danced around it, stopping behind Lina. "Go for it."

Lina pushed her remaining chips in front of her and split the aces — not because Alex had told her to, but because it was the right thing to do. The dealer flipped a queen over her first ace.

"Good girl." Alex gave her a high-five as the dealer paid out the blackjack. "One more!"

No sooner had Lina scooped up her winnings than she was dealt a four on her second ace. *"Merde."*

"I love it when you talk French." Alex motioned to Lina's cards. "No problem. Take another."

"I'd rather hold and let him bust." Lina declined the draw. Alex leaned over her shoulder, and Lina felt Alex's breath on her neck, maybe even the brush of her lips.

"You just passed up a seven," Alex whispered. The dealer laid a seven in front of the next player. Lina waited for an "I told you so," as the dealer drew to seventeen and took the other half of her chips. But Alex just scooped up her winnings, tipped the dealer, and headed for the door.

"It was still the right move," Lina defended, as Alex climbed into the Miata.

"I never said it wasn't." The attendant pushed the door closed behind her.

Lina hurried around to the other side. "But you're thinking it." She slid behind the wheel and adjusted the mirrors. "I know you are." Alex counted her money silently. "You just did well because you spend so much time in your laptop casino."

Alex smiled. "Maybe."

"That's nothing to be proud of."

"If you say so."

"You were right about the seven though."

"Yes."

"So, I suppose you think that proves intuition is better than reason?"

"Card counting."

"Excuse me?"

"Card counting is better than reason."

"It's also against the rules."

"True." Alex's body pushed up against the seatbelt as she stuffed the cash into her back pocket. Lina struggled to keep her eyes on the expressway.

"I love Natalie Merchant." Alex turned up the volume on the radio. "She cuts right to the chase. No bullshit."

"Is that how you see *yourself*?"

Alex leaned her head out the window. "On my good days."

It had been a long time since Lina had had a good day. "Alex..."

"Alanis Morissette is like that too. Her songs'll just rip your skin off. No mercy. That's honesty."

"Honesty is unmerciful?"

"Not so much unmerciful, more like...unfettered by consequences."

"Thick skinned."

"No, just the opposite. Truth demands intense sensitivity. And sensitivity demands intense truth."

"That's illogical."

"Most truths are, Dr. Spock."

"So good of you to remind me, Counselor Troi."

"Hey, the first Star Trek was way better than the second."

"You're joking."

"No way. It had that great sense of campy-ness. The second one takes itself way too seriously. Always on the high moral horse."

"Weren't you just building a case for morality?"

"Is that what I was doing?" Alex lit a smoke. "I just figure you gotta be able to laugh at yourself, you know?"

Lina glanced at her reflection in the rearview mirror. She didn't find much to laugh about. "Alex . . ." She turned down the radio.

"Yeah?"

"I . . . you . . . I . . . don't know which exit to get off of from here." Her bid for courage failed again.

"If you take the next exit, we could cruise over to the wharf for a bit."

"Everything would be closed."

"That's the coolest time. We could walk down by the water, hang out on the pier. We'd have the whole place to ourselves."

"That's not safe."

"Are you kidding? The only people we'd run into would be cops. They do the coffee-donut number down there." She laughed. "And show up at the most inopportune moments."

Lina didn't even want to consider what that meant. "I have to get some sleep. I've got class first thing in the morning."

"Your call." Alex tossed her cigarette out the window. "The third exit up will get us home."

117

"Thanks." Lina turned the radio back up, loud.

Alex drummed the dashboard all the way home. "That was a blast." She hopped out of the car and pulled Lina into a hug.

"I enjoyed it very much." Lina held her arms stiff and waited for Alex to let go. She watched the moon escape from a purple cloud overhead. "Thank you for inviting me."

"You owe me one."

Lina stepped back, pretending to stretch. "One what?"

"That's up to you." Alex stuck her keys in the front door. "Surprise me."

Lina twisted a finger through her dark hair. "I will."

"Don't forget." Alex pushed the door open with her knee.

"I won't." She started across the damp grass toward the cabana.

"By the way," Alex called behind her. "That dress . . ." Lina stopped and turned. Alex gave her a thumbs up, then disappeared into the house.

11

"One of those . . . glow-in-the-dark plastic tubes, please." She handed the vendor five dollars, then five more. "Make it two. One purple, one green." She held them up against the dark sky, twisting them into a double helix. A flash of a dream sprinted through her mind and quickly disappeared.

"Lina?" Someone tapped her shoulder from behind. She turned to find Pam, tank-topped and short-shorted. "I thought I recognized you. It's always strange to see students out of context."

Lina glanced up the hill at Alex. She wasn't sure why. "Am I out of context?"

"Well, you don't have your book bag and you *are* wearing shorts, so I'd have to say yes."

Lina looked down at the cut-offs Alex had lent to her, insisting that she couldn't wear a skirt to the park.

"Actually, these aren't mine."

"That doesn't surprise me. Who're you here with?" Lina pointed up to the knoll, where Alex was helping Nathan spread a quilt while Claire and Sean set out snacks. "Family?"

"Oh, no. I mean, they are family, but not my family." Lina felt an odd discomfort at the disavowal. "I look after the boy. He's Nathan Elliason's son."

"The provost?"

Lina nodded. "Who are you here with?"

"Me, myself and I. Two friends were supposed to come, but they got in a fight with each other and both bagged out. You'd think at least one of them would've come, but they had to out-stubborn each other or something." The first firecracker exploded against the black sky. "Anyway, I wasn't gonna miss it."

"Would you like to join us?"

"Sure, if it's OK with them."

"I'm sure it would be fine." Lina led Pam up the hill and conducted the introductions.

"Hey, you got one of those fire sticks." Sean pointed to the green glow-in-the-dark tube, which peeked from Lina's front pocket.

"For you." She handed it to him.

"Look what I got." He swung it in the air, creating a trail of light.

120

Alex's eyes tracked the glow. "I love those."

"Say thank you, darling." Claire tapped Sean.

"Thank you," he offered dutifully.

"You're welcome, honey." Lina pulled the second tube from her pocket. "One of your very own." She held it out to Alex.

"Mighty thoughtful of you." Alex wrapped it into a circle and held it above her head. "Angel."

"You're welcome." Lina reached for a wine cooler and offered it to Pam. "Drink?"

"Sure, thanks." She popped it open and lifted it. "Cheers."

Alex lifted her bottle. "Cheers. Have a seat." She tapped the quilt. Pam dropped to her knees beside Alex, as the sky erupted into whistling green and red swirls.

"Whoa!" Sean's eyes flashed with sparkling light. "Did you see that?" He tugged on Nathan's shorts.

"See what?" Nathan pulled Sean onto his lap and winked at Lina. "Have a seat." He shifted to make room.

"PLG, darling?" Claire offered Lina a finger sandwich as she sat down.

"PLG?"

"Pepperoni, lettuce and gouda. I made them myself."

"You cooked!" Lina laughed. "Thanks."

Another round of explosions splashed the sky with tiny purple and gold orbs. Alex and Pam both said "awesome" at the same time, then, thoroughly amused with themselves, clinked bottles. Sean followed suit, tapping his Coke can against Lina's. "We're twins!"

Lina didn't respond, too busy staring at Alex.

"Would you like a wine cooler too, dear?" Claire asked.

"Oh . . . no, thank you." Lina was embarrassed to have drawn attention. "I'm fine . . . being twins with Sean." She forced a smile.

"Well, I'll have one!" Claire popped open her third, as a sphere of flickering blue light overtook the sky. Alex and Pam clinked bottles again, and again after every explosion that followed.

Finally the sky burst into a deafening shower of red, white, and blue stars that brought the crowd to its feet. Lina took Sean's hand as Nathan shepherded them through the mob that poured down onto the street.

"That's my bike." Pam motioned to a Yamaha near the corner. "So, this is where I get off."

"That's yours?" Alex veered over to the bike without waiting for an answer and hopped on.

"Want a lift home?" Pam held out her helmet. "I've got an extra."

"Definitely!" Alex looked over at Claire and Nathan and pretended to rev the engine. "That cool with you guys?"

"It's fine with me." Nathan nodded. "What do you think?" He took Claire's hand.

"Well, I suppose she remembers how to ride from boarding school." Claire winked and turned to Alex. "Don't you, dear?" Lina couldn't help smiling at the expression of horror on Alex's face. "Just make sure you keep that helmet on your head."

"No problem . . ." Alex struggled to regain composure.

"Thanks for a wonderful evening." Pam shook

hands with Claire, then Nathan. "See you in class." She waved to Lina.

"Goodnight." Lina waved back, as Pam slid in front of Alex and pulled off down the street.

Lina pulled the sheets off her bed for the third time. They wouldn't lie properly, and Alex still wasn't home. It was only a twenty-minute ride, and they'd left over an hour ago. She tried to feel worried, or even angry — anything except hurt, which, for some reason, was all she felt.

When she finally heard the roar of the bike coming up the driveway, she flipped off her lights and ducked into the window alcove. She watched as Alex hopped off the bike and pulled her helmet off. There was some conversation, which Lina couldn't hear, and Alex played with her hair a lot. Her glow-in-the-dark tube was wrapped around her neck, and she pulled it off and wrapped it around Pam's. More conversation, and then Pam made a U-turn around Alex and drove off. Alex looked over to the cabana as though she might head that way, but instead she pulled her keys from her shorts and disappeared into the house.

At last the sheets lay properly, and Lina went to sleep.

12

COLD STONES SHOWER DOWN AND TOWER UP INTO
BLACKNESS, LADDERING TALLER THAN JACK'S
BEANSTALK INTO THE LAND OF COVENS. THE
QUEEN OF HEARTS STANDS GUARD, FRAMED IN
A WINDOW THAT BECOMES A CAGE AND TRAPS
HER. SHE LAUGHS A CRY THAT SPLITS THE
NIGHT, SPILLING BLOOD FROM ANCIENT
WOUNDS. JAGGED NEON FLASHES SPIRAL DOWN

AND CORKSCREW INTO THE GROUND. DOUBLE-
FACED PLAYING CARDS ERUPT FROM THE
CHASM AND SPRAY JUMBLED SCENES THAT
INDELIBLY MARK THE DISTANT HORIZON.

Lina had no assignments due for Cognitive Psych
lab, and so, for the first time, she decided to skip
class. She dropped Sean off at Tai Chi for Tots, then
planned out her morning over an espresso at
Starbucks. Propped on a stool by the front window,
with her dark-ringed eyes reflected back at her in the
glass, she could not deny that the nightmares had
become unbearable. Long on exhaustion and short on
ideas, she devised a search of the World CompuLine
to dig up anything she could find on dreams.

It had also been two weeks since she'd last
e-mailed her father — and though he hadn't seemed
to notice, she wanted to send a note assuring him
that all was well, and that she would soon be making
arrangements to return home. She hadn't thought
much about that, and she jotted a reminder on her
napkin. "Search airline database — collect flight information — HOME."

She pulled only halfway up the driveway and
parked, hoping to slip into the cabana unnoticed. But
as soon as the patio came into view, so did Alex,
posted in her usual pool-side spot. A stack of books
was piled on the ground to her left, and to her right
was a pitcher of orange juice, her Camels, and a
Zippo.

"Don't you have Pam's class this morning?" Alex

typed on her laptop without looking up. A phone cord stretched along the patio and in through the French doors.

"I have other business to attend to this morning." Lina didn't slow as she passed.

"I'm on the second draft of my paper. Nathan gave me some tips to restructure it. He was impressed."

Lina turned. "I'm impressed too."

"You haven't even read it."

"I'm impressed that you wrote it."

"Hmm." Alex sipped her juice. "Low expectations."

"That's not what I meant . . ."

"Yes it is. But that's cool. I probably deserve it."

"No, you don't. I'm sorry."

"Like I said, no problem. It's too nice a day to hassle. You should put on a suit and come out."

"I need to work on my computer."

"It's a laptop. It goes where your lap goes."

"I need access to my phone line."

Alex gestured toward the bay windows. "Those aren't painted shut are they?"

They could be really quickly, Lina thought.

"Just pull your cord through there. Smart college girl like you can figure that out . . . or maybe you skipped that class too?"

"Right. Fine." Lina backed toward the cabana. "I'll put on my swimsuit and be out in a bit."

Alex resumed typing. "If you insist."

Lina dawdled in her room for as long as she could, then stepped into her Speedo and pulled the straps up over her shoulders. She looked at herself in the mirror and twirled around a few times, then slipped a shirt on. It didn't seem right trying to work in a bathing suit. It would be difficult enough with Alex there.

Coated with Sunblock 35, Lina ran her phone cord through the window and settled into a lounge chair across the pool from Alex.

"Now, isn't this better than being holed up in that room?"

"It's very pretty out." Lina booted up her computer and dialed Online. Out of habit, she signed on as NXTDOOR and began composing a letter to her father. As she mailed it off she realized her mistake. *"Mon Dieu . . ."*

"Problem?" Alex looked up from her work.

"Oh . . . no."

"Cos if you have a problem, I could help you out. I'm getting pretty good at this."

"No, no problem. Thank you, though. I just typed in the wrong return address." She quickly clicked on the "Unsend" icon.

YOUR MESSAGE HAS BEEN UNSENT

"Writing to Dad?"

"Yes, I am."

"He ever write back?"

"Irregularly. But yes."

"That's good." Alex looked back to her screen. "I'm searching through some files from PBS. That's public TV here."

"Sesame Street."

"Yeah, Sesame Street. And lots of other amazing shows. They have transcripts of them, some even have pictures, and you can just download them. Then, a little cut and paste, and voila — instant term paper.

"With proper references and citations, of course."

"Of course. Just like Xeroxing articles back in the stone age, only now you don't have to waste time at the library."

"I enjoy the library."

"Me too, I guess, sometimes. But it's so . . . quiet. Plus, you can't get a tan there."

"An important consideration."

Alex scooted up in her chair and slid two fingers under the elastic of her bikini bottoms. "You get high?" She pulled out a cigarette-sized joint.

"No. I mean I have, but I don't."

"Helps me concentrate."

"It always had the opposite effect on me."

"I would've guessed you'd never touched the evil weed."

"Actually, I prefer, preferred, hashish."

"You know where to get any?"

"No. That was long ago and far away." Except for those couple times out back at Corridors . . .

Alex took a hit and held her breath before she spoke. "My friend Denny grows this stuff out on Vancouver Island. But it smokes a lot like Hawaiian."

"A connoisseur."

"It's radically expensive, but he gives it to me for free." I bet, Lina thought. "I saw that look." Alex took another hit. "And you're wrong. That's why I like him. He has no interest in me. I mean, he has *little i* interest, you know, but not *big I.*"

Lina recognized this rating system. It put Denny into roughly the same category as Zack. "I follow. But don't you agree that little i's have a tendency to become big I's?"

"Well, sure. I think the best big I's start as little i's. But it seems like usually that leads to no 'I' at all." Her green eyes darted in thought. "Hey, that can be taken two ways, can't it? 'No I at all...'"

"You're stoned."

"Getting there, but it's still true. Don't you think?" She pulled a ball-point pen from behind her ear and jotted something on her hand.

"You've got things hidden everywhere, don't you?"

"I just gotta make a note of it so I can read it later, when I'm not baked, and see if it really means anything. Sometimes these little snippets lead to incredible lines of thought." She slid the pen behind her ear. "Other times I don't have a clue what I was thinking. But you gotta follow through and take a shot at it." She took a last hit off the joint and squeezed it out between her fingertips. "The sky is majorly blue." She slid down in her chair.

"You're not going to get any work done now, are you?"

Alex sat back up. "Oh, I am. Definitely." She adjusted her laptop screen. "See. Working." She began to type.

Lina stared at the school of purple guppies swimming across her own screen, trailing a GET BACK TO WORK banner. She clicked off the screensaver and checked her watch. She still had an hour before she pick up Sean, enough time to resend her e-mail and track down a few flights. As she moved her cursor to the SWITCH SCREEN NAME icon, a small box appeared in the center of her screen.

RUSHIN: HEY ZACKO! SURPRISED TO FIND U
    ONLINE AT THIS HOUR.

She glanced nervously across the pool as her stomach twisted into a knot.

RUSHIN: WHAT A PLEASANT SURPRISE.
RUSHIN: IT'S THE MOST BEAUTIFUL DAY HERE
    TODAY.
NXTDOOR: HERE TOO. WHY AREN'T YOU OUT
    ENJOYING IT?
RUSHIN: <--- POOL-SIDE AS WE SPEAK! AND U?
NXTDOOR: JUST TAKING CARE OF SOME
    BUSINESS.
RUSHIN: ME 2. WORKING ON A PAPER.
NXTDOOR: OBVIOUSLY...
RUSHIN: I MEAN I WAS, BUT NOW I HAVE A
    REALLY NICE BUZZ AND JUST FEEL LIKE
    EXPLORING.
NXTDOOR: I UNDERSTAND.
RUSHIN: SAW SOME AMAZING FIREWORKS LAST
    NIGHT. DID U GO 2 ANY?
NXTDOOR: I DID. QUITE SPECTACULAR.
RUSHIN: CAUGHT A RIDE HOME ON A FRIEND'S
    YAMAHA. MADE ME THINK OF U.
NXTDOOR: NICE OF YOU TO SAY.
RUSHIN: IT'S TRUE. IT WAS A BLAST. WARM
    WIND, LOTS OF STARS.
NXTDOOR: SOUNDS ROMANTIC.
RUSHIN: IT WAS, I GUESS. SHE DID HIT ON ME.

NXTDOOR: SHE?
RUSHIN: YEAH.

Alex lit a cigarette, and Lina considered joining her.

NXTDOOR: AND ...
RUSHIN: AND NOTHING. SHE SAID SHE THOUGHT
    I WAS HOT AND DID I WANT TO GO OUT
    DANCING. I SAID THANKS BUT NO.
NXTDOOR: YOU SOUND QUITE CASUAL ABOUT IT.
RUSHIN: NO BIG DEAL. NOT THE FIRST TIME
    IT'S HAPPENED. PROBABLY NOT THE LAST.
NXTDOOR: ANY INTEREST?
RUSHIN: NOT SO FAR. BUT I'VE LEARNED NOT
    TO RULE ANYTHING OUT.
NXTDOOR: WHY?
RUSHIN: IT ONLY TEMPTS FATE TO DROP U IN
    THAT SITUATION.

The thought crossed Lina's mind that this might be the perfect opportunity to reveal her identity. She could chalk it up to fate and synchronicity. Alex would like that.

NXTDOOR: AND WHAT IF I WERE A WOMAN?
RUSHIN: WHAT IF?
NXTDOOR: WOULD U BE INTERESTED?
RUSHIN: I'M ALREADY INTERESTED.
NXTDOOR: YOU ARE?
RUSHIN: WISH U WERE HERE NOW.
NXTDOOR: YOU DO?
RUSHIN: MY SHOULDERS ARE GETTING BURNED.
    COULD USE SOME OIL.

NXTDOOR: :::RUBBING OIL ON YOUR SHOULDERS, DOWN YOUR ARMS:::

RUSHIN: MY BACK IS BURNING TOO . . .

NXTDOOR: :::SPREADING IT DOWN YOUR BACK, AROUND THE SIDES OF YOUR BELLY:::

RUSHIN: DON'T WANT ANY TAN LINES. WOULD U UNDO MY TOP?

NXTDOOR: :::UNHOOKING THE STRAPS AND SLIDING THEM DOWN:::

RUSHIN: ALL THE WAY.

NXTDOOR: :::DROPPING IT TO THE GROUND:::

RUSHIN: MUCH BETTER. LOVE TO FEEL THE SUN BEAT DOWN ON MY BREASTS.

NXTDOOR: HOT?

RUSHIN: ENOUGH TO MELT ICE! A TITILLATING IMAGE, DON'T YOU FIND IT . . . ?

NXTDOOR: DO YOU HAVE ANY?

RUSHIN: ICE?

NXTDOOR: ICE.

RUSHIN: NO.

NXTDOOR: CAN YOU GET SOME?

Lina meant only to glance at Alex, but their eyes met. Alex smiled casually. "How's it going?"

"Good." Lina nodded. "Fine."

"I'm gonna run into the house for a Coke. Want anything?"

Lina smiled. "No, thank you." She looked back to her screen.

RUSHIN: HANG ON A SEC.

Alex stood and stretched her long body, then sauntered into the house. She appeared unsuspicious. Self-conscious, if anything. Lina slid down in her chair and watched a triangle of gulls cross overhead. The sky *was* majorly blue.

"Want a mouthful?" Alex veered back across the patio, carrying a tall glass of Coke — on the rocks. She held it out to Lina.

"Yes. No. Yes." Lina forgot the question, distracted by the thin swatch of green bikini at her eye level. "Sorry." She reached for the glass. "Please."

"You dig into my stash while I was gone?" Alex chuckled.

"Excuse me?"

"Never mind." Alex stared down at her. "So, you gonna drink that or what?"

"Yes." Lina took a sip so cold that it burned her back teeth. "Ahhh . . ."

"Was that 'ahhh' as in pleasure, or 'ahhh' as in pain?"

"A bit of both, I'm afraid."

Alex looked like she was about to say something, but didn't. She reached for the drink. "Back to work for me."

She spun around to leave.

"An illustrated woman . . ."

Alex stopped and looked back. "Illustrated?" Lina pointed to the tattoos, which she'd just noticed. "Oh, those. I was wondering when you'd spot them."

"They're very discreet."

"It was a personal thing. Sort of a gift to myself. You disapprove?"

"Well, no . . ." Lina shifted uncomfortably. "I don't."

"Liar," Alex half-joked.

Lina mounted a brief internal debate, then pulled

aside the collar of her polo shirt and lifted her hair. She could feel the sun against the back of her neck, a strange sensation.

"Whoa . . ." Alex moved in for a closer look. A silver crescent moon was curled within an inverted black triangle at the nape of Lina's neck. She reached and gently touched it. "Are you a good witch or a bad witch?"

Lina's whole body tingled. "I don't understand."

"What's the symbolism? The triangle-moon thing?"

"It's just a design." Lina dropped her hair and pulled her collar back up. "It's meaningless."

"No way. It means something. You wouldn't have done it otherwise."

The leaves swayed suddenly on their branches, sending shadows dancing across the cobbled patio. The beach ball lifted and spun across the pool — red, yellow, red, yellow.

Alex's hair wrapped wildly around her face. "Whoa."

Lina tilted her head back and closed her eyes. "The breath of the wind."

Alex looked impressed. "Nicely put. Where'd you steal it from?"

"I think I just made it up."

Alex dipped a finger into her drink and swirled the cubes. "Full of surprises, aren't you?"

Lina sat up and shifted her laptop down her thighs. "I suppose that raises my esteem in your eyes?"

"Not in the least. It just confirms my suspicions . . ." Alex's voice trailed off as her eyes locked on Lina's computer.

Lina's breathing stopped as the enormity of her

blunder snapped into recognition. She was afraid to look at the screen, and her mind scrambled in search of damage control.

Alex puffed her cheeks and puckered her lips like a fish. "Get back to work."

Lina glanced down and caught sight of the purple guppies completing their lap of her screen. "Right..." She heaved a breath. "Right."

Alex traipsed around the pool and settled back into her lounge chair. Lina slipped a hand under her shirt and rubbed her stomach in circles. She felt nauseous, dizzy, like the glare of the sun was burning through her eyes. She wanted to go back inside. Inside her small room, inside her small self. But Alex was typing again, and Zack would have to be resuscitated.

RUSHIN: I'M BACK. U STILL THERE?
NXTDOOR: LONG WAY TO THE FRIDGE?
RUSHIN: SORRY. GOT THE ICE!

From the corner of her eye, Lina saw Alex fish an ice cube from the glass.

NXTDOOR: ACTUALLY, I'M RUNNING A BIT SHORT
    ON TIME.
RUSHIN: IT'S ON MY BELLY. MELTING ALREADY.
    IT'S SO COOOLD!
NXTDOOR: REALLY, I HAVE TO TAKE A RAIN
    CHECK.
RUSHIN: IT'S DRIPPING DOWN MY SIDES. WON'T
    TAKE BUT A MINUTE TO LICK IT OFF...U
    WOULDN'T LEAVE A GIRL WET, WOULD U?
NXTDOOR: NOT UNLESS I HAD TO.

RUSHIN: COLD FEET?
NXTDOOR: IT'S NOT THAT.
RUSHIN: THEN U R A TEASE.
NXTDOOR: JUST BAD TIMING.
RUSHIN: U MAY NEVER GET ANOTHER CHANCE.

Lina looked across the pool and knew this might be true. Her head was pounding.

NXTDOOR: SORRY. REALLY.
RUSHIN: TOO BAD.
NXTDOOR: CAN WE TALK LATER TONIGHT?
RUSHIN: DON'T THINK SO.
NXTDOOR: ARE YOU ANGRY WITH ME?
RUSHIN: MORE LIKE DISAPPOINTED. I'M
    GENERALLY ON THE OTHER SIDE OF "NO."
NXTDOOR: I HAVEN'T SAID NO.
RUSHIN: IT'S COOL. I KNOW THIS ROUTINE.
NXTDOOR: YOU DON'T UNDERSTAND.
RUSHIN: I DO, AS MUCH AS I NEED TO.
NXTDOOR: WHEN CAN WE TALK AGAIN?
RUSHIN: I'LL LOOK FOR U.
NXTDOOR: I'LL LOOK FOR YOU TOO, PROMISE.
    I'M SORRY.
RUSHIN: BYE FOR NOW.

Lina typed in GOOD-BYE and got a flashing message that Alex had already signed off. She pretended to keep typing, not wanting to arouse suspicion, but Alex was already collecting her belongings and heading for the house.

Despite the meticulousness of her hunt, Lina knew she had just shot herself in the foot. She tried to convince herself that Alex would appreciate the gesture, if only she knew the truth. But if Alex knew the truth, Lina would be in worse shape than Zack already was. She could barely wrap her mind around such a convoluted thought — and that night, when she finally closed her eyes against the long, dark fingers that clawed at her walls, her dreams were fierce and unforgiving.

13

Lina was chopping a potato into cubes when a tiny green race car careened in from the hall and crashed into the stove. This had been going on all morning, and she was getting short on nerves.

Sean barreled into the kitchen, grinning. "That's the fastest car in the world!"

Lina stooped and picked it up. "Eggs and hash browns for lunch today, OK?" She rolled it back to him along the counter top.

"Some for Alex too?"

"Alex is sleeping."

"Uh-uh." He shook his head emphatically. "Mom and her are out, and Mom said they would come home when the little hand is on the twelve and the big hand is on the . . . thirty."

"You mean at twelve-thirty?"

Sean nodded and checked his Super Mario watch. "On the six," he corrected himself.

Lina grabbed two more potatoes from the basket and began chopping. "Where did they go?"

"Shopping for the party. Are you going to the party? I can't go cos it's past my bedtime and I have to stay at Grandma Gracie's. But you could go. And she lets me stay up late anyway."

"I don't know anything about a party."

"It's not yet. It's later." He held up several combinations of fingers. "In that many days."

"We'll see." Lina scooped the cubes into a frying pan and set the burner on low.

"Alex likes me now." He held the car in the air and spun its wheels. "She gave me this. It's the same car as she has. I'm twins with her now!"

Lina was surprised to find herself slightly stung by his comment. "It's very nice."

He dropped to his knees and rolled the car around him in circles. "Alex has a boyfriend."

Lina busied herself cracking eggs into a bowl. "Omelette or scrambled?"

"She told me."

"Do you want your eggs scrambled or in an omelette?"

Sean stopped playing and looked up at her. "Omelette."

"Listen." She wiped her hands and knelt in front of him. "I have an idea. You put the car away for a

139

little while and help me set the table." Sean's expression was less than enthusiastic. "This one can be for Alex." She stood and pulled a plate from the cabinet.

"OK!" He took the plate and headed off purposefully into the dining room. Lina distractedly poured the eggs into the frying pan. "Merde." She poked at them with a spatula as they spread and sizzled across the potatoes.

"Potato eggs?" Sean giggled behind her.

"I thought I'd try something new." She flipped the whole concoction like a pancake. "Mish-mash hash. You'll like it very much." She handed him another plate.

"Mish-mash hash!" He marched back into the dining room, and Lina heard the click of Claire's heels crossing him in the hall. "We're having mish-mash hash," he announced.

"It smells wonderful, darling."

"What the hell's mismatch hash?" Alex grunted.

"Mish-mash," he corrected.

"Alexandra Wilder, watch your language please." Claire breezed into the kitchen.

"That's Alexandra Zhivago Wilder," Alex yelled from the hall. "Remember?"

Claire rolled her eyes in Lina's direction. "A little too much togetherness, I'm afraid."

Lina tidied the counter. "Lunch will be ready in just a few minutes."

"I think I'll just fix a tomato cocktail and retire to my room."

Lina recognized the euphemism. It meant an afternoon of Bloody Marys and talk shows in bed.

"Very well. Would you like me to bring you up a tray?"

"Oh no, darling. I just bought a new dress for the party and well, you understand, taste makes waist." She furled her brow. "I did tell you about the party, didn't I?"

"Not that I recall."

"It isn't until the twenty-eighth, that's a Saturday, but you can never be too prepared. We're counting on you being there. I ordered for forty, and we'll have music. Calypso, probably. Nothing like the limbo after a few Mai Tais." She closed her eyes and tilted her head back. "The stories I could tell you."

"I'll plan to stop in." Lina turned off the burner.

"Wonderful, darling. I'm sure Alex will be happy to have a playmate." Claire pulled a gallon bottle of tomato juice from the fridge. "Ta-ta." She disappeared down the hall.

Lina scooped the hash into a serving bowl and tried to shake the "playmate" comment. She realized she hadn't heard Sean in awhile, and called his name up the stairs.

"I'm in here." His voice came from Alex's room.

Lina went to the door and leaned in. "Lunch time."

Sean curled his fingers into claws and growled. "I'm starving." He charged past her into the hall.

Lina glanced around the room. She felt strange being in there. It had been a long time. "There's plenty for you too."

"No thanks. I need some down time."

"Rough morning?"

"Claire still throws me over the edge sometimes.

Especially in public." Alex slid the window open and lit a cigarette. "I finally had to just take a time out and go my own way."

"She took you shopping and you left her alone?"

"No need for you to be offended. She wasn't. Both of us like it better that way. She can do her thing and I can do mine."

Lina couldn't justify having any further investment in the issue. "Well, I hope you enjoyed your *thing*." She turned to leave.

"Actually, I did. I paid a little visit to Madam Kalderas." Lina stopped in place, but didn't look back. Alex laughed, self-satisfied. "I *knew* you'd have a problem with that."

Lina forced herself to turn. "I have no problem with that."

"The whole idea irks you. I can tell." Alex swung a leg out the window and sat on the sill. "It's not like you just don't believe in it, it's like you hold some personal vendetta or something."

"Believe me, you're reading something into nothing. I think it's *you* who are irked by my not lending credence to that . . . that . . ." She waved her hands in the air. "That patchwork of loosely stitched perspectives you call a world view."

Alex puffed her cheeks and blew a smoke ring in Lina's direction. "That was a mouthful."

Lina started down the hall. "You don't need my approval."

Alex slid down from the sill and followed behind her. "I don't need your disapproval either, you know."

Lina rounded the table and took a seat beside Sean, who looked back and forth several times between her and Alex. "This is yummy." He laid his head flush with his plate and bulldozed a forkful of hash into his mouth.

Lina glared at Alex. "So why did you even bother to tell me about it? You know my position."

"I thought you might find it interesting. I was trying to give you some credit for being open-minded. My mistake."

"I find that rather sarcastic, coming from a spiritual person such as yourself."

Alex leaned on one hand against the arched entryway. "You never let up, do you? You go right in for the kill."

Sean pushed his plate out in front of him. "Finished." He stood and pulled his race car from his pocket. "We could go play in the hall. It's a racetrack. We could take turns."

"You go on ahead." Lina rubbed his shoulder. "I'll join you in just a bit." He dropped to his knees and rolled the car along the floorboard, out into the foyer. Lina spooned some hash onto her plate. "We shouldn't speak like that in front of him."

"Always worried about other people's impressions." Alex smirked. "True to form."

"Concerned with no one but yourself. Per usual." Lina forced down a mouthful of cold hash and grimaced.

Alex shook her head, and Lina somehow knew what she was about to say before she heard her say it. "We sound like an old married couple."

Lina slowly chewed and swallowed. "I don't despise you that much."

"That's really comforting." Alex approached the table. "Really, really comforting."

Lina looked up at her, and something about the afternoon sun made Alex's eyes look greener than she'd expected. Every gold and crimson fleck seemed painted just so, just for her, just for that chance glance upward. "Hash?" was all she could think to say.

Alex smiled deviously. "You have some?" Lina tilted the serving dish toward her. "Oh that. After that face you just made? Yeah, right."

"It's not bad." She poked at a clump of eggs. "The microwave could give it a whole new life."

"I'm game." Alex reached over the table and grabbed the dish. "I'm working on a Butterfinger and three Snapples so far today."

Lina followed Alex into the kitchen. "So . . ." She grabbed a Brillo pad and busied herself with the frying pan. "What did the mind reader have to say?"

Alex set the microwave. "Lots of things. It was kind of weird, actually."

"How so?"

"I picked the 'Tree of Life' tarot deck for my reading. The cards are round and the designs are really amazing. She makes them herself. No two decks are exactly alike."

"But they are all politically correct, fat-free, and have never been tested on animals."

Alex hopped up on the counter and let the comment slide. "So there are four 'Daughter' cards in the deck, one for each suit. They symbolize a youth-vigor-subconscious-waxing-moon type thing. You know?"

"I'm with you," Lina lied.

"Power. Transformation. Disinhibition."

"Sounds like trouble."

144

"They each mean somewhat different things, of course, but when I pulled my cards, I drew all four of them. All four. Moralia said that in the whole time she's been doing readings that's never happened before."

"Moralia?" Lina noted the first-name basis and felt her insides twist into a knot.

"Yeah, that's her name. She's got the wildest black hair and the darkest eyes. Beautiful woman, and really intense."

Lina scrubbed the pan with a vengeance. "So what did the ravishing mountebank say is the titanic significance of getting four daughters?"

"What's a mou . . . mountainbike?"

"Never mind."

"I didn't say she was ravishing."

"Never mind. Continue with your story, please."

"Well first, get this, she asked if I was pregnant."

"And?"

"And I said 'Only with possibility.' "

"Maybe she knows more than you."

"Impossible. I haven't been with a guy in . . ." Alex closed one eye in thought. "Over a year."

"Shouldn't the great and powerful Moralia have known that?"

"She's a card reader, not a spy."

"What about Christmas in Denver?" Lina couldn't believe she'd just said that. "Claire told me." She shrugged.

"Denver was just an excuse to not come home."

"You didn't go?"

"I went. Skied for days. But the guy was just a friend."

"And Montana?"

145

"Montana?"

"Camping?"

"Camping means camping. What's it to you, anyway?"

"You brought it up."

"I did."

"The pregnancy thing."

"Oh, right. Anyway, then she looked at some of the other cards and asked me if I was in love."

"That old-fashioned precursor to pregnancy."

"I guess. But not in this case."

"I don't understand."

Alex hopped down from the counter and strolled over to the side door. "There *was* someone that came to mind . . ." She sounded surprised herself. "But pregnancy is definitely not a part of that scenario."

Lina put the long-clean pan aside and shut off the tap. "Very cryptic."

"You think?" Alex stared out the door. "I bet you could figure it out if you tried."

Lina resented being fogged with innuendo. "Frankly, I'm not all that interested." She began unloading the dishwasher to prove her point.

"That's cool." Alex stepped outside. "Don't think about it, then." She kicked the door closed behind her and sauntered down the hill toward the dock.

14

Lina had lost count of how many days and nights she'd been holed up in her room, venturing out just enough to not be missed at work or school. She'd managed to avoid all but the most superficial contact with Alex, who seemed generally oblivious to her absence — and she took comfort in the fact that her life was beginning to look familiar again. Except for the piles of dirty clothes that patched the floor, the undone assignments stacked on her desk, the bags and boxes bearing logos from every fast-food drive-thru within a five mile radius.

Today she'd distracted herself with thoughts of home. She'd posted a list of plane flights by the window, squared her account at the university, and arranged to have her final grade report mailed to Athens. She'd even had the "big talk" with Sean, who, to her dismay, became convinced she was leaving any minute and spent most of the evening in tears.

"I could say good-bye to you before you go to the airplane," he said yet again as she tucked him into bed.

"Of course you can, honey." She brushed a curl back from his forehead, and felt angry with herself for having upset him in the interest of calming her own anxiety. "That isn't going to happen for a little while though. I just wanted to talk with you about it."

"We could play one more game of Safari Trek. Just one more, OK?"

"We can play more, but not tonight. We agreed to ten-thirty bedtime, remember?"

"I went to sleep from . . . little hand on the five to little hand on the . . . five, six, seven, *eight*."

"Right. That's why you got to stay up until now. Don't push your luck." She heard her father's voice as she said that.

Sean rolled onto his belly and curled up. "You'll come and get me in the maawwwniin?" His words were consumed by a yawn.

"Just like every day, buddy." She flipped off the light. *"Bon soir."* He was asleep before she reached the door.

Whispers of saxophone drifted up the stairway as Lina made her way down. She picked up speed through the darkened hall, vowing not to let her eyes drift from straight ahead as she passed Alex's door — and she would have kept that vow, had the most enchanting sight not rebelliously danced across her peripheral vision.

Alex's room was pulsing with gold-white candle light and through the slit in the door Lina could see her spinning in slow circles, back and forth across the hardwood floor, in and out of view. She was wrapped in a white towel and hugged some sort of dark fabric in her arms. Lina was mesmerized, and couldn't say how long she'd been standing there when Alex asked.

"So . . ." Alex leaned against the door frame, un-self-conscious. "Did you want to come in?"

"No." Lina shook her head. "I didn't. I mean, I don't. I mean . . . no." She took a step back. "Thank you."

Alex half-smiled. "Do you honestly find me so intimidating?"

Lina's defenses snapped to attention. "I don't find you intimidating in the least."

"Well, what is it then?"

"What is what?"

"This whole approach-avoidance thing. It started when we first met."

"I don't know what you're talking about."

"Honestly?"

Lina hated direct questions — they left far too little room to maneuver. "Is that what you bought for the party?" She motioned to what she now could make out as the suit in Alex's arms.

"Just come in, OK?" Alex hugged the suit against her body and backed into her room. "I promise not to bite. Unless you want me to, that is." Lina didn't budge. "Joke, Lina. That was a joke."

"You didn't answer my question."

"It's a long story. Come in, alright? I'll give you the Reader's Digest version."

Lina didn't understand the reference, but her whole body ached at the sight of Alex's bronzed skin against the white of the towel. That she understood. "If you insist." She followed Alex into the room.

Alex sat at the edge of her bed and patted the sheet beside her. "Make yourself comfortable."

"I'm fine, thanks." Lina paced the room, ostensibly engrossed in the candles but actually just trying to shake off nervous energy.

"Gives the place a religious feel, don't you think?" Alex sounded nostalgic. "The only thing I gained from my Catholic upbringing was a love of ritual. No need to throw out the baby with the baptismal water. You just gotta make it your own, you know?"

Lina rearranged a grouping of red candles and sat beside them on the window sill. She could see her room across the pool. "Tell me about the suit."

Alex laid the black slacks across her legs and held the jacket out in front of her. It was burgundy, tuxedo-style, with a black silk lapel and cuffs. "It was my dad's. Sort of."

"Sort of?"

"I bought it for him. Must've washed a hundred cars to get the money. It was for his birthday. He *looked* medium, but I guess he was large. It looked so funny the one time he tried it on. Mom ran and got the camera. I still have the pictures."

"And the suit."

"He didn't take it when he left. He packed kind of quick. Didn't have much room in his suitcase and all."

Lina looked at Alex, and through a strange distortion of light, she saw the girl from the living room portrait looking back at her. "Was there a big scene?"

"Oh, lots of them. But not that day." Alex folded the jacket and set it on her lap. "That day it was just . . . quiet. Very, very quiet."

Lina dripped red candle wax onto her palm and sculpted it into a ball. "How old were you?"

"Twelve." Alex lay back on the bed and fixed her eyes on the ceiling. "Almost past that stage where you think your dad is God . . . but not quite past it. How old were you when your mom died?"

Lina tried to mask her surprise. "Excuse me?"

Alex rolled over and looked at her. "Claire told me."

"Of course . . ." Lina poured more wax into her palm. She hated this conversation, and had spent a lifetime finessing its avoidance and fine-tuning its variations. "Five. I was about five."

"That would be tough." Alex adjusted her towel. "Do you think it's harder when the person's dead, or when they're alive but you never get to see them or talk to them?"

"I imagine they're equally difficult, just in different ways."

"I think it'd be easier if my dad were dead. I spent a long time pretending he was. Do you think that's an awful thing?"

Lina shrugged. "Do you?"

"No. Yeah. Sometimes. I think it's a natural thing. Dr. Pelke said it was."

"Therapy."

"You bet. Dad split in the morning and by afternoon I'd been signed up and delivered to Dr. Pelke. They actually made *her* break the news to me officially. Gotta love it."

"People act strangely when they're in pain."

"Still, they're accountable for their behavior and the weight of the freight left behind. That's what Dr. Pelke called it, 'the weight of the freight'."

"I'd think a woman like you would leave accountability in the hands of karma."

"Oh right, you don't even believe in that stuff."

"But you do."

"What do I know?" Alex sat up. "I'm young. Still unfolding, like a rosebud."

"Steeped in bullshit. You'll grow fast." Lina tossed the wax ball at her. "So, you just keep that as a souvenir?" She motioned to the suit.

"Of course not. I wear it. Well, I did a couple times." She ran her palm over the lapel. "Mom hates it."

"Because it belonged to your father?"

"Nothing that deep. I think it went more like . . ." She contorted her face into a stern expression. "It is inappropriate for a girl of your caliber to be parading around in men's garments."

Lina smiled at the image. She could picture Alex in the suit, hear Claire's tone. "Which, no doubt, made you want to wear it all the more."

"Oh no, this wasn't that type of thing. It means too much to me to use that way." Alex's eyes traveled Lina's body, and she got a strange look on her face. "Put it on." She held out the suit.

Lina curled back against the window and shook her head. She wanted Alex's gaze off of her, but the intense green eyes only flickered gold in the candlelight and held their stare.

"C'mon." Alex slid from the bed and slowly approached. "I know you have it in you."

"Why should I?"

Alex moved in close, and Lina caught the scent of marine bath salts rising from her skin. "Because I want you to." She pressed the suit against Lina's body.

Lina felt like her skin was burning up. She could feel her heartbeat through her entire body. "No..." She ducked around Alex and backed toward the door.

Alex didn't turn around. "That's cool," she whispered.

Lina shuffled nervously by the door. "I just don't think it would be a good idea."

Alex leaned her forehead against the window and stared into the night. There was a protracted silence before she spoke again. "Don't sweat it." She laid the suit on the ledge and turned to Lina. "It's almost time for me to go online anyway. I've been having some really hot chats." She pulled a pack of Camels off her night table and looked at Lina through narrowed eyes. "Did I tell you?"

Lina was sure Alex knew she'd never mentioned it. She wrapped her fingers around the door frame and pitched her voice to a disaffected tone. "No."

"Doesn't surprise you though." Alex rounded the bed and crossed toward her. "Does it?" Lina backed into the hall, heart pounding. Alex continued past, without pause. "Touchy . . ."

"Alex . . ."

"After all . . ." Alex swept an arm across her cluttered desk, sending a collection of empty Snapple bottles crashing into the trash can. "I told you there *was* someone . . . and that pregnancy wasn't part of the scenario." She lifted her laptop and held it against her chest. "Seedless as a Sunkist, and every drop as sweet."

"The sterile lover . . ." Lina heaved a breath, but Alex's continued stare denied relief. "I should have known."

"Yes." Alex laid the laptop on her bed. "You should have."

Lina couldn't read Alex's look and wasn't sure she wanted to. "I won't keep you any longer." She started slowly backwards down the hall. No response came — just the tinny, techno-echo of Alex's computer dialing back online. And then the sound of footsteps coming toward her.

"Midnight snack." Nathan toasted her with his Cup-A-Soup. "Are the children settled in?" He chuckled.

Lina shifted nervously. "All is well."

"You know, I spoke with my brother earlier today. He might be coming for a visit this fall."

Lina wasn't sure where this was leading. "That's nice."

"I'm excited by the prospect of seeing him. He's been stationed abroad since . . . well, before Claire and I were married. Sean is his godson, and he's only ever seen pictures of him."

Lina inched casually toward the front door. "That must be difficult for all of you."

"Him most of all. But he won't make the trip until Phillip, that's his partner, can get time off too." Nathan spooned a mouthful of soup and stared at Lina. "The point is, I respect him for that. I miss him like hell, but, well, I wouldn't make a trip like that without Claire either. It's the same thing, if you know what I mean."

Lina wondered if Nathan meant even more than he was saying. "I think I do."

"I hope you do." His tone was serious. "It's the same thing is all I'm saying. At least in my book."

Lina was lost for words. "I . . . understand."

"I'm glad." Nathan nodded and headed up the stairs. "Goodnight."

"Goodnight . . ."

Lina crouched low and sped her bike down the steep hill. Her hair whipped behind her in the night wind, and for an instant, there was nothing else. Nothing but freedom and solitude and warm air that carried the scent of the bay. She wished she could bottle it like a salve or wrap it into an amulet for safe-keeping. But as soon as she tried to grab the moment, it disappeared — leaving her alone in the moonless night, confirmed in her belief that all is transient.

She pulled up in front of the club and chained her bike to the stop sign. Women spilled along the sidewalk, buzzing with the carefree energy of midsummer. She felt their eyes on her as she wove through them, keeping her own eyes straight ahead. Someone held the door open, and music pounded at her as she stepped into the flash of swirling of lights.

"Come ..." A porcelain-skinned woman took her by the hand and lured her into the mass of bodies. The steamy heaviness of musk rose all around her, and she felt the press of flesh as she wrapped into the crush. "Move with me." Her hips were being urged into a gentle sway, a figure eight, an orbit that seemed to pull her from the ground. Fingers traced down her chest, and an aromatic smoke coiled around her. "Breathe." There was a press against her lips, the sizzle of burning hash as she drew in deeply, a caress that slipped and tumbled into a kiss. Then hands, traveling the skin of her thighs, tucking beneath her skirt ...

"I can't." She pulled back, or thought she had until she felt the graze of fingertips against her crotch.

"You're wet." The breathy voice warmed and chilled her simultaneously. "So am I." She felt her hand being guided into the crevice between blue-jeaned legs, then the burn of friction. She closed her eyes and felt her body rushing toward the point of no return. And then ... a strange slipping. A flipping inside out. Her mind suddenly alone in a dark space, disconnected from the flesh and fluid abandoned in dance below. The body tightened, drew a wave of nausea through it, called her back. But she was trapped. Speeding through an endless blackness in vacant silence, until all semblance of self disappeared.

"Can I help you?" A voice summoned from above, and a hand touched her shoulder. "Are you hurt?" Her spinning mind funneled back into her body like water whirling down a drain. She could feel the night's warm air against her skin, the cool scratch of pavement beneath her. She looked up into eyes that were dark as the emptiness from which she'd just returned, and she glimpsed her own reflection looking back at her.

"I'm fine." She struggled to her feet, and did not take the woman's hand when it was offered.

"I know you." The woman pulled her dark, wavy hair behind her head.

"Yes. I've passed by your . . . place . . . many times."

The woman gestured behind her, and Lina realized where she was. The sign flashed red against the night. "Madam Kalderas — Palms and Cards Read."

"A little boy's usually with you."

Lina scanned for her bike, but it was nowhere in sight. "Yes."

"Your son?"

"Thank you for helping me." She stepped back. "But I have to go now."

"It's very late. I can borrow a car if you need a ride —"

"No . . . thank you."

"Come in for a reading sometime, then. No charge."

Lina nodded. "Goodnight."

"A very good night." The woman stared at her intently, but Lina quickly turned away. She focused on the sound of her own footsteps against the pavement, as she made her way down the street briskly and without looking back.

15

A SILVER CRESCENT SCYTHE PRETENDS TO BE THE
MOON AND BLEEDS ITS LAST LIGHT INTO THE
NIGHT. GRAVE DARKNESS SURGES. THE SLEEP-
ING TOWER WAKES, BLINKING OPEN ITS CAT-
EYE-YELLOW WINDOWS AND EMITTING CONCEN-
TRATED CONIFORMS OF STARE. JAGGED IONIC
FLASH- CRACKS STRIKE AT IT FROM ALL DIREC-
TIONS, BLOWING ITS STACK AND CRUSHING ITS
KEYSTONE, CAUSING IT TO CONCEDE, COLLAPSE,
AND RE-CONSTITUTE. AN ANGEL-CRONE
EMERGES FROM THE MIX, LAUGHING SALTY

TEARS DEEPLY AND FOR REASONS UNKNOWN.
SHROUDED IN DARKNESS, SHE DENUDES —
DROPPING HER CAPE TO EXPOSE HER CAPER,
UNWEAVING TANGLED TAPESTRIES OF FATE.
DARK AND BURNING LIKE THE SOLAR ECLIPSE,
SHE CAN NEITHER BE WATCHED NOR IGNORED . . .

The patio was already crowded with well-dressed guests mingling over exotic drinks, by the time Lina got herself together enough to venture out of the cabana. She traveled swiftly around the pool toward the house, declining hors d'oeurve after hors d'oeuvre from handsome young waiters eager to serve her.

"I'm so glad you decided to come, dear." Claire veered toward her and kissed the air in her general vicinity.

"I wouldn't have missed it." Lina forced a smile, recalling how many times in the past week it had been made clear that she was expected to put in an appearance.

"There's an open bar in the den." Claire swung her Mai Tai toward the house, splashing some on a passing waiter. "And I'm having these boys set up another by the pool. I think it's a good idea, don't you?" She pulled a tiny pink umbrella from her drink and stuck it in Lina's hair.

"It . . . looks like a wonderful party."

"And it's only just begun." She toasted Lina and sipped her drink. "Alex is just inside, in the den. She's with John Rutherford's son. Nathan's golfing buddy. John, that is, not the son. They live just next door." She swung her Mai Tai toward the east gate. "The two of them have been in there a long time. Alex and John Junior, that is. In the den, I mean."

She leaned in conspiratorially. "Maybe he has a friend . . ." She winked.

Lina was dumbfounded. She felt like the victim of some cruel cosmic joke — and promptly reminded herself that she didn't believe in such things. "Probably," she conceded.

"Darling, I must go." Claire waved across the pool. "The president of the university is here and I haven't even said hello to her yet. Do be a dear and excuse me." She disappeared into the crowd.

Having spoken with Claire, Lina figured she had fulfilled her obligation and could surely be absent for the rest of the evening without being missed. She had no interest in sharing Mai Tais and country club stories in the den with Alex and John Junior, and so made her way back toward the cabana feeling eager to sink into a bath and crawl into bed. But instead she was greeted by a line-up of buzzed party-goers who wrapped around the side of the cabana, each as eager as she was to use her bathroom. She cut through the azalea bushes and detoured along the periphery of the patio to avoid being seen. The steel drum band was just beginning their set, and the muted notes seemed to follow her as she trekked down the landscaped path toward the edge of the property. The scent of the water drifted up to meet her, and she realized she had a headache only then as it began to dissipate. She thought she saw something spark against the darkness of the water, and as she approached the dock she could see what looked like tiny flames dotting the cabin of Nathan's boat. She climbed on board and cupped her hands against the window for a better look.

"We meet again." Alex's voice came from the back

deck. Lina turned, but was too startled to respond. "How'd you know I'd be down here?" Alex smiled.

"I wasn't . . . I didn't . . ." Lina noticed that Alex was wearing a dress. "Is there a priest here?"

Alex pinched the edges of her purple sundress and curtsied. "Wanna come in?"

"Three's a crowd."

"You're with someone?"

"No games, OK? Just for once. I know about John Junior. I didn't *want* to know, but that's just how it goes with Claire."

Alex's face hardened. "You are so totally off." Her voice was cold and quiet. "J.J.'s like a brother to me. And what the hell is it to you anyway?" She turned and disappeared behind the cabin.

"Alex . . ." Lina heard a door slam and came around the back deck. She pulled the cabin door open and stepped in. Her eyes strained to adjust to the candlelight. She could make out the leather couch and recliner, the small bar, the glass dining table. "Alex?"

"You've got a lot of nerve." Alex stood in silhouette against the far window. "And yet you're a complete coward."

Lina felt her stomach knot at the truth. "There's something you should know . . ."

Alex stopped pacing. "There's something I do know."

The boat rocked with the rising tide, and Lina steadied herself against the glass table. "You do?"

"Um-hmm. You watch me through my window."

"Oh, Jesus . . ."

"Don't you think I can see you too?"

162

Lina took several steps back. "No ... I mean yes ... but ..."

"But you won't make love to me on your computer."

Lina slumped into the chair. This couldn't be happening. She felt mortified. And relieved. "How long ..."

"Since the day you didn't." Alex crossed the cabin and stopped just in front of her. She reached for the dimmer switch and turned the lights up.

Lina stared down at the floor. "I'm so ..."

"Knowing it was you," Alex crouched in front of her, "... made me wet." She placed a hand beneath Lina's chin and gently lifted it. "Look at me." Lina glanced sideways to avoid eye contact. "I was glad to know it was you. I felt totally screwed up about the whole thing. I'd be talking to Zack all night, then dreaming about you till morning." She pushed Lina's hair back off her face. "Once I knew it was you, it made sense."

"You saw my computer screen."

"Actually, I didn't. Except for those purple fish things. But your face went totally white and then red when I looked at it. I knew you were up to something. And then when Zack suddenly bagged out on me ..." She shrugged. "I could've killed you. Except that I wanted you so goddamn bad."

"So all this time ... that night in your room ..."

"That night I knew for sure. Before that, there was still the infinitesimal chance that I might be totally whacked. But then you got that same crazed look on your face when I handed you the suit."

"You should've said something."

163

"Your game, your rules, your move." Alex rested her hands on Lina's thighs. "And you owe me the answer to a question . . . Zack."

Lina shrunk back. "Don't call me that." She stood and stepped around Alex, who used the chair to pull herself up.

"You never told me what scares you."

Lina leaned forward against the table. The glass felt cool against her palms. "That's . . . personal." She felt Alex come up behind her. Fingers slid into her hair, lifting it from her neck.

"I'm about to make love with you." Alex's lips pressed against her ear. "*That's* personal."

Lina whispered, "That's what scares me."

Alex stepped back, then took Lina by the shoulders and turned her around. "I'm user friendly." She smiled just slightly, then took Lina's hands and held them against her cheeks. "Monitor . . ." She pulled them gently down her neck, around the curve of her breasts, across her belly. "Keyboard . . ." She tucked them between her legs, gathering her dress between her thighs. "Mouse . . ." She spoke the words right into Lina's mouth, as their lips brushed together. "How scary is this?" she whispered.

Lina wasn't sure if she said "terrifying" or just thought it. Her body ached, and she groped for the dimmer switch. "I can be anyone you want me to be." She darkened the room.

Alex reached around her and turned the light back up. "You already are."

Lina felt naked. More naked with her clothes on than she'd ever felt with them off. "What if it's Zack you really want?"

Alex slowly unbuttoned her sundress and let it

drop to the floor. She wore nothing underneath, and Lina was stunned to see the fullness of a body she'd only glanced at guiltily for months. "I want you both."

Lina laughed awkwardly. "A *menage a trois,* of sorts."

Alex moved closer, and Lina felt the soft touch of hands sliding beneath the silk of her blouse. "French . . ." Alex pulled the shirt up over Lina's head. "Drives me crazy." She held the fabric against her face and inhaled.

Lina crossed her arms over the lace of her bra. The room was hot, but she felt chilled. She startled at the touch of Alex's belly against hers, the feel of skin against skin. The sensation felt intense and unfamiliar — and she realized for the first time that her encounters with women, though numerous, had always involved one partner remaining clothed. And darkness. And scripted interchange, if any at all.

"It's not me you're afraid of, you know." Alex draped her hands over Lina's shoulders and played with her hair. "You were afraid way before you ever met me."

Lina kept her arms crossed in front of her. "It's that obvious?"

"Anyone that looked could tell." Alex smiled. "And I've been looking."

Lina's whole body tightened under the penetration of Alex's green eyes. Her mind struggled to detach itself, but her skin was on fire and escape was denied. "I . . . think I'm in love with you." The words left her lips without permission.

"You say that like it's a bad thing." Alex took Lina's face in her hands. "Is it?"

"I suppose not..." She felt the gentle press of Alex's lips against hers.

"You suppose not?" Alex eased Lina backward toward the table. "I see I have my work cut out for me."

Lina felt the sudden chill of glass against her back and shoulders. Then Alex's fingers... traveling up her belly, wrapping around the lace of her bra, pulling it downward. She felt the soft slide of lips against her nipple, the tickle of hair against her shoulders, the weight of Alex's body settling against hers. A chrome light dangled above, drawing her attention, slowly transforming itself into a bare blue bulb swinging from a grate in a dark corridor. "Wait..." Lina wrapped an arm around Alex and used the other to push herself up. "Not like this."

Alex continued to hold her close. "Not like what?"

"I want to see you." She brushed a tangled curl from Alex's face and looked into her eyes. "I want... to touch you."

Alex took her by the hand. "I thought you'd never ask." She slid her off the table and led her to the back of the cabin, where a dark hall opened into a small bedroom. Lina stood by the door as Alex lit a row of candles on the night table, then climbed onto the bed and propped open the window hatch. "Would bed be too personal?"

The scent of the bay filled the glowing room and Lina's approach was easy and unencumbered. She knelt on the bed beside Alex, leaned forward and kissed her deeply. She called Alex's name softly between breaths, and maneuvered cooperatively as Alex's hands slid the remaining clothes from her body.

"Wanna get meta-physical?" Alex playfully pinned Lina down.

"I'm beginning to see the merits." Lina ran her hands up Alex's spine and felt a lifetime of armor melting away.

"The feel of you is incredible," Alex whispered, as Lina wrapped her in strong arms and rolled her onto her back. "So intense, surprising . . . I never imagined . . ." Her words faded into a soft moan, as Lina's lips covered her breasts with tiny kisses that trailed moistly down her belly.

"I owed you a surprise." Lina dipped her tongue between Alex's legs. "I am good on my word."

Alex leaned her head back and moved against Lina's mouth. "You're good all right."

Lina watched Alex's body rise and fall, stretching with an elegance she hadn't seen before. It was liquid and fiery at the same time, and she was drawn into its rhythm. She felt like she'd made love to Alex a thousand times before. And like she'd never made love before at all.

"I'm right on the edge," Alex whispered. "Let me see your eyes." She wrapped her legs around Lina's back and urged her gently upward till she could look fully into her eyes. "Dark like the night." She pressed both hands against the small of Lina's back and moved against her. "Show me what's in there."

Lina gripped the sheets and anchored her body to Alex's. Their bellies generated a sweat that slid them easily against each other, rocking together, until Lina heard her name called . . . her real name . . . and Alex shook beneath her in intense bursts that pounded through her body.

"Alex . . ." Lina arched in muscle-deep response to

the energy pulsing through her. Her body clamped and opened with each rise and fall of Alex's body, and she stretched to kiss her as she crested and released and subsided into aftershocks against Alex's damp skin.

They held each other through the night, sleeping lightly in the moments between caresses and tangles of legs and arms — and as the sky slowly layered with the colors of morning, Lina knew a conversation needed to be had. But Alex's hair was sweetly curled around her face, her lips were moist and full, her eyes still struggling to stay open. The conversation would have to wait until another time

"You have that most rare and amazing talent . . ." Alex curled on her side and looked at Lina. "Of being able to make love and fuck at the same time." She smiled. "A girl could get spoiled."

Alex's candor caught Lina off guard. "I . . . don't know what to say."

"It was a compliment." Alex propped herself up on her elbows. "Say 'thank you' "

"*Merci.*"

"Ohh . . ." Alex rolled over and laid her face against Lina's belly. "I warned you about French."

Lina tugged Alex's hair at the roots. "*Dit moi lait encore,*" she whispered.

Alex rose to her knees and straddled Lina's belly. "You're a tease."

"*Nous somme un à l'autre.* "

"Now look what you've done." Alex took Lina's hands and pressed them between her legs.

Lina gripped the inside of Alex's thighs and pulled her forward till she was just above her face. She ran her fingers up Alex's body, cupping her breasts, gently squeezing her nipples. *"Ha que tu et chaud."* She dipped her tongue into the rosy folds of skin, licking slow strokes up and down their length. *"Je t'enbrasse."*

Alex came almost instantly, collapsing slowly backward against Lina's body, trying to catch her breath. "I want to be inside you." She sat up and rubbed her wetness against Lina's belly. "So far inside that I can't find my way out."

Lina ran her hands up Alex's thighs. "I'd like that."

"You would, would you?" Alex smiled slyly. "Then ask me."

"Ask you what?"

"Ask me to fuck you." Lina felt her face go flush. "You can't say it, can you? You can *do* it . . . damn can you do it . . . but you can't say it." Alex laughed. "That's sweet."

"I can say it."

"So say it."

"That's juvenile."

Alex smirked. "See?"

"Fuck. OK?"

Alex leaned forward till her face was just inches from Lina's. "Say 'fuck me'," she whispered.

Lina smiled. "Fuck you."

Alex twisted around and slid a finger easily inside

her. "Good enough . . ." She pulled it slowly out, then pushed two in its place. "Good enough."

Alex's scent rose in the steam and diffused, as hot water sprayed down Lina's body and swirled into the drain. Their rendezvous had grown frequent — frenetic and furious and sometimes several times a day — but still Lina burned with the constant ache of desire. Making love in the light was addictive.

Today in class she'd unexpectedly caught the scent of Alex on her fingers, and had watched the hands of the clock jerk with agonizing slowness toward the moment she could return home and feel Alex against her. She'd pedaled home with all the gusto of the Tour du France, saying "fuck me" with every stride — and had been only barely fazed by the nod of Madam Kalderas as she zoomed past the storefront. Alex was waiting for her in the cabana, naked and in bed as planned, and few words passed between them as they hungrily reunited. Agreeing to meet Alex again later that night, Lina put in a few distracted hours of study for finals, which were now only a week away. The days and nights were slipping by quickly, and so much remained unsaid.

Lina had barely gotten into Alex's room when Alex wrapped around her and pressed her back against the door. "I've been missing you." She felt Alex's hands slide under her skirt and around her thighs, pulling her close. "I think your contract says you're supposed to be in my arms at all times," she whispered.

Lina fought the urge to let her growing wetness

distract her from her mission yet again. "I need to talk with you about something."

"I know."

"You do?"

"I've been meaning to talk to you too." Alex bounced playfully against her. "But it's so hard to want to, when I can be kissing you instead." She teased Lina's lips with her tongue.

Lina caught herself eyeing the bed, and reined herself back onto her task. "Alex..."

Alex peeled herself back with a half-pout. "Old iron will." She gestured toward the bed. "Take a seat in my office, then." Lina eyed her suspiciously. "Have no fear." Alex rolled her computer chair out from under her desk. "I'll be way over here." She spun it backward and straddled it.

Lina smoothed down her skirt and took a seat on the bed. Alex stretched her legs out and rolled her chair back and forth, which for some reason seemed so erotic to Lina that she forgot her well-rehearsed speech and instead fumbled for words. "There was... a reason... I came here. To... Seattle."

"Right." Alex winked. "With you so far."

"And... that's what I need to talk to you about."

"I understand, and I wanna to talk to you too." She rolled the chair closer to the bed. "You've got, what, maybe two weeks left of school?"

"One."

"And then you're done with us and outta here, right?"

"I wouldn't put it that way."

"Of course you wouldn't. That's part of your charm. But it *is* what you're saying, isn't it?" Alex slid forward and touched her knees to Lina's. "You did what you came here to do, and it's time to make a graceful exit. No waves. As planned."

"There are . . . factors . . . that have nothing to do with you."

"If that's what you need to tell yourself."

"It's the tr . . . truth." Lina knew she was skating on thin ice when it came to the truth.

"Let's make it simple. You *are* leaving, right." Lina nodded. "Then I have only one thing to say." Lina bit her lip and prepared for the worst. Alex rolled right up against the bed between her legs. "Don't."

Lina had armored herself for attack from outside, but instead found herself helplessly melting from within. "You're leaving anyway. Before me."

"Stay here. Be here when I come home for the holidays. Come visit me at school. I'll fly you out."

"I can't."

"You can, but you won't. And I don't get it." Alex grabbed Lina's hands and squeezed them. "I'm in love with you. You know that. I know you do."

Lina wasn't sure whether she knew that or not. She hadn't much wanted to think about it. "It's not a matter of that . . ."

"And you're in love with me."

Lina couldn't help herself. "Life's not as simple as it looks at twenty-one."

Alex wedged her heels against the floor and pushed her chair back. "The only reason I'm not gonna be *furious* about that remark is that I know you're just running from the real issue."

All the issues were starting to merge for Lina at this point. "It wouldn't be right to abandon my family like that. I do have a sense of responsibility, you know. It's an important thing."

"That's total upside-down, back-assward, hypocritical bullshit." Alex shook her head in disapproval. Or was it disappointment? "Sean's your family. I'm your family. We, this family here, are your family. Don't you get it?"

"My family's in Athens."

"Your father's in Athens. And you've got a ton of convincing to do if you want me to believe there's much *family* going on there."

"He is my family. He's all I've . . ." Lina stopped before complicating the matter, but Alex's eyes told her she'd already gone too far.

"You don't know what family is."

Just one more push and Lina knew she could be out of there. "Look who's talking."

Alex's eyes narrowed and teared. "Let's say our good-byes now then, OK?" She stood and walked to the door. "Good-bye." She pulled it open and gestured for Lina to leave.

Having successfully wrangled the invitation, Lina made her exit without a word.

16

A TICK-TOCKING TOWER SCRAPES AGAINST A
   STORMY SKY, TOLLING THAT TIME HAS COME TO
   AN END. TRANSFIGURING INTO A CROW-EYED
   CRONE WITH MOONSTONE EYES, IT SWOOPS
   DOWN AND OUTSTRETCHES A DARK HAND TO A
   TINY SUPERNOVA, WHO COCOONS BACKWARD
   AND IMPLODES TO HIDE WITHIN BLACK HOLE-
   NESS. SYLLABLES RAMBLE VAINLY FROM THE
   CRONE'S ROSE LIPS AND ARE VACUUMED INTO
   SILENCE — MUCH ADIEU ABOUT NOTHING. A

HEARTBEAT SLOWS TO SELF-STIFLE IN THE
SAFETY OF AN ENDLESS NIGHT, KNOWING THAT
OUTSTRETCHED HANDS ARE STAINED WITH
BLOOD AND FOREVERMORE UNTOUCHABLE.

Still sweat-drenched from the nightmare, Lina's skin chilled into shiver as she sped her bike down the hill. The flashing neon sign fractured into red beams through her tears, and she pointed herself directly into their center. One way or another, this had to come to an end.

She chained her bike to a streetlight and rapped on the storefront window. "Hello. Hello, it's me." She moved to the door and rang the small buzzer. "Hello. Please. Is anyone here?"

A slash of light spilled into the room from the back hall, and a tall figure came toward her through the darkness. Lina wiped tears from her eyes, as the woman unbolted the door and pulled it open.

"You've come." Madam Kalderas motioned for Lina to come in. "I wasn't sure you would."

The small room smelled faintly of incense, and Lina felt her stomach turn. She crossed to the center of the room and waited. She heard the door close behind her, then a small lamp was switched on, casting a mustard glow against the maroon walls. Plants hung everywhere and a Siamese cat lay curled by a space heater in the corner. It opened one blue eye to look at her, then returned to sleep.

"Have a seat." Madam Kalderas sat down at the table and pulled the other chair out for Lina. She stacked three decks of cards across the black velvet cloth. "Your preference?"

Lina stood beside the table and eyed the cards. "Those." She pointed to the round ones. "And I'll stand."

"Whatever makes you comfortable." She removed the other decks from the table. "You're a night owl." She smiled. "I am too." She handed Lina the cards. "Hold these. Shuffle them if you like, then give them back to me when you're ready."

Lina handled the cards awkwardly, wondering how she'd know when she was "ready." No particular moment struck her, so she cut them once and handed them quickly back.

"You keep them. You're unfamiliar with the tarot, am I right?" Lina nodded. "Then my feeling is we should do an open-faced spread. Do you agree?"

"It's all the same to me."

She gestured to the table. "Spread them here, face up." Lina did as she was told, while Madam Kalderas lit a candle and mumbled some incantation she couldn't make out.

"Now, look at the images, and pick four cards that strike you in some way. Don't try to decode the symbols, and definitely don't be distracted by the titles. Just reach for whichever ones hit you on a gut level. Be spontaneous."

Lina focused her mind on the cards with great care, certain that such a choice should not be so frivolous as suggested. Starting at the beginning of the deck, she pushed each card aside with her finger, studying them one by one, looking for any sign to choose that particular image. There were elements of shape and color that attracted her, but nothing seemed willing to reveal itself to her. When the card with the upside down figure made her laugh unexpectedly, she decided that was sign enough. "This one." She slid it aside, then returned to her analysis. She shifted past Temperance, The World, The Sun, and then hit an image that fired every nerve in her body. She broke into an itchy sweat, and lifted her collar to wipe her forehead.

Madam Kalderas lifted the card. "This one . . ."

Lina paced around the table. She didn't want to choose the card, whose tower spired up into a lightning bolt that blew its top off. It somehow seemed too self-revealing. But she had come this far, and so she silently forced her eyes back down to the remaining cards. The Daughter cards caught her attention as they passed, but she refused to choose them, continuing instead until she yet again hit an image of towers. Two towers this time, flanking a silver moon.

"La Lune." Madam Kalderas quickly slid the card aside. Her dark eyes flickered with candlelight.

Lina acquiesced to her fatigue and took a seat in the small, wooden chair. She did not touch the cards, but only scanned them with her eyes. The Chariot looked appealing, with its rider majestically positioned above two steeds. There seemed an element of control in it that might counterbalance the cards she'd already stacked against herself. "This one." She pointed.

"Very interesting." Madam Kalderas removed the unchosen cards from the table. "This represents you. *Le Pendu*." She placed the Hanged One in the center of the black cloth.

"*Tres bien*," Lina said sarcastically, and in French without realizing it.

Madam Kalderas smiled, then became more

solemn as she laid The Tower above and to the left of The Hanged One. She spoke in a whisper, *"La Maison Dieu* represents the past."* She kept her eyes on the table and placed a third card directly opposite the second. *"La Lune* represents the present."* She took the final card and centered it below "The Hanged One," completing an inverted triangle around it. *"Le Chariot.* The Future."* She traced the outer triangle with her fingers. "These form a cloak around the inner figure, but they are not the figure itself. So let's deal with this one first." She pointed to The Hanged One.

Although hanging upside down, the figure looked upright from Lina's position across the table. "It looks better from this direction."

"Of course it would. It's instinctive to want to turn the Hanged One right-side-up, except that's exactly what she doesn't need."

"What did she do to deserve such torture?"

"It feels like torture at first, and naturally she's struggled against it. But resisting just distracts her from the view, and the view is the whole point."

"What's the point of seeing everything upside down? That's not reality."

Madam Kalderas smiled as if Lina had said something very amusing. "It's the same reality, just from a new perspective. Fate wants you to see things from a different angle, and so it's holding you captive till you do. See." She pointed. "The figure's hands are bound behind her back. She's in the grip of fate."

"I don't believe in fate. It's an excuse for lack of self-direction."

"Fate doesn't mean predestination, it's more like the landscape we navigate through. Our little Hanged

One here was blind to certain parts of that landscape, but only because of her own stubborn way of looking at it. The fairies flipped her over to set her free. To shake things up so she can get moving again."

"Fairies?" Lina's tone was filled with sarcasm.

"The Three Sisters of Fate. Past, Present and Future. The Triple Goddess. The Three Divine Mothers."

"I get the idea."

"They're also represented by the triangle." She again traced the inverted outer triangle. "The delta. The Holy Door. A female symbol, as I'm sure you've noticed."

Lina hadn't. "Right."

"The Hanged One dangles between two trees, and her head dips into a crevice in the earth. She's being reacquainted with her roots in Mother Nature, and also with her own unconscious nature. At the same time, the feet she used to stand on now face up to the big blue sky, seemingly useless, right? But notice how one leg is bent at the knee, crossing the other to make a four. That number means completeness. Even though she's upside down, she's actually in better shape than she's ever been." Madam Kalderas looked at Lina, filled with seriousness. "Or at least the opportunity's there for her to be, if she stops letting fear distract her and takes a look at what's right in front of her."

"Is that editorial?"

"Would it make it any less true?"

Lina remembered using the same line on Alex, which agitated her even more. "So, what about this one?" She pointed to the Tower card.

"The Tower of Destruction..." Madam Kalderas tilted the card toward the candle. "Also called the House of God."

"So, is it good or bad?"

"There's no such thing really. It's always both, and neither. It just depends how you look at it."

"Spoken like a true fortune-teller. Vague and noncommittal."

"It's not really fortunes that I tell. It's more like circumstances and possibilities."

"Well, the sign out front says 'Fortune Teller.' "

The woman smiled. "It costs too much to write 'circumstances and possibilities' in neon. I checked."

Lina refused to be charmed out of her irritation — especially with The Tower shimmering in the candlelight, sending chills all the way through her. "What does it mean?"

"It's a stroke of liberation. Think of the tower as a person. It's strong, protective, a good place to retreat and observe from. But it's also a prison of sorts. It's rigid, thick-skinned, inaccessible." She pointed to the lightning bolt. "The lightning knocks off the top of the tower, which would be the head, so some light can get in. It leaves the person feeling a bit shocked, pun intended, and exposed and confused."

"That sounds definitively bad."

"Not in the view of the Hanged One, who can see things upside down and *use* the light that's pouring in."

"For what?"

"To take a look at herself. From the inside, where it used to be dark. Once the lightning hits, whatever's inside becomes illuminated and therefore conscious. The change is immediate and inescapable. The intuition is set free of the intellect. That's the liberating part."

"What if liberation isn't what they wanted? What if they were just fine the way they were?"

"The unexamined life is not worth living. And the unlived life is not worth examining."

"But that's all the past, right? Not now."

"The card is in the 'Past' position, yes." She looked at Lina curiously. "Does it seem to resonate with your present?"

Like an earthquake, Lina thought. "I didn't say that."

Madam Kalderas rocked her chair forward on two legs. "All right, then. Let's take a look at the next one." She glanced down at the cards. "More towers, but of a different nature. Interesting..." She lifted the Moon card. "Are you having nightmares?"

Lina felt as if the wind had been knocked out of her. "How ... what makes you think that?"

"Well, a few things. For one, the Moon Goddess is known to be the giver of dreams, the revealer of hidden mysteries." She pointed to the blue pond in the foreground. "Then, there's the reflecting pool. The Cauldron of the Deep, in gypsy folklore."

The reference made Lina cringe. "What does it mean?"

"It's like a mirror that traps the soul, confusing it with its own memories. That's why I asked about nightmares." She waited for a response, but none was forthcoming. "The towers again, with the moon and the reflecting pool ... it's like you're struggling in the present with things from the past. But of course, that's what this card is really about."

181

"I thought you said these towers were different."

"They are. Look." She pointed. "See the guardian creatures on either side? They're intended to bring fear, but only as a test of courage. Before you can advance past them and between the towers, you have to sink down into the pond, into the murk of a lifetime's memories, and make the final settling of accounts. It's called The Dark Night of the Soul." She stared at Lina intently. "But it has to be done."

Lina felt like she was being prodded, which only strengthened her resistance. "To get to the moon? What's the point?"

"Freedom. Always freedom."

"From what?"

"Fear. The fear that comes from not really knowing yourself, from using all your energy just to keep yourself hidden. Besides . . ." She smiled. "The moon is the realm of feelings and eroticism and sexual instinct."

That was enough of that. "What about the last card?"

"The future." Madam Kalderas ran her fingers gently over the card. "The Chariot that carries us home."

"That one makes sense." Lina felt a sense of calm and validation in knowing the future lined up with her plans.

"What do you see when you look at it?"

"The woman driving it looks calm and in control. Like she knows where she's going."

"Indeed. She's riding toward her destiny." Madam Kalderas looked at Lina with an expression that seemed almost proud. "But the real journey's going on inside her. The Chariot's just a vehicle that helps her get where she's going. Like anything and anyone in the world, it always boils down to learning about yourself. Coming home to yourself."

Lina liked her own interpretation better. "Maybe it just means she's going somewhere and it's the right choice."

"It's not exactly a matter of choice — it's more about grace, and understanding. She neither drives, nor is driven." She pointed to the two horses that pulled the chariot. "Notice, no reins."

"So who's in control?"

"In a way, the Chariot itself. But that's because it's a part of her. It's the guiding force inside her. It means she's no longer being controlled by ideas and energy outside herself. She's brought them within her, sorted through them, picked the ones that really fit her." Madam Kalderas locked her dark eyes on Lina. "And as she travels, her deeds reveal who she is ... to herself, and everyone else." She reached across the table and put her hand on top of Lina's. "Welcome home."

Lina stiffened. "You know ..."

She nodded. "I do."

Lina jerked her hand away. "Why didn't you say something?"

"You didn't want me to. You weren't ready."

Lina stood. "Who says I'm ready now?" She felt a wave of rage and terror and incredible sadness wash over her. She wanted to run, felt like she was suffocating, gasped for breath. It seemed like almost a dream when the woman reached to embrace her.

"Let me ..."

"Don't you dare." She pinned herself back against the wall. "You have no right."

"Then why did you come here? Certainly not for a card reading."

"I came here for answers."

"Did you get them?"

Lina felt tears begin to stream down her cheeks. "Why can't I sleep at night? Why do I feel like I'm always running and something's right there..." She choked the words out through her sobs. "Right there behind me, in front of me, next to me, in my skin... always wanting something and it's too much..." She slid down the wall into a crouch. "Black towers over my bed and lightning so close it's in my mouth and I can taste it... and then I'm suffocating and the moon is like a scythe and I'm burning up..." She wrapped her arms over her belly. "And everything's dark... dark like your eyes, dark like a hole — " Lina suddenly heard her own words wrap back around her.

"Dark like my eyes..." The woman knelt on the floor in front of Lina. "And like yours." She reached and touched Lina's face, lifting it until their eyes met. "What's true of the ocean is true of the drop."

"I'm not like you." Lina turned her face away with a look of disgust. "There's a lot of things I am, but I'm not like you."

"I guess you'd know that better than me." She leaned back and sat on the floor. "You were the same way back then. Hard to accept that from a five-year-old."

"What's that supposed to mean?"

"It means I knew you were right. As much as I didn't want to, I did."

"Right about what?"

"About staying with your... staying in Europe."

"Versus?"

"Leaving . . . with me . . ."

"I never had that option."

"Honey . . . you did."

"That's a lie. At least admit it was a despicable thing to do."

"It was a despicable thing to do." She spoke in a whisper and swallowed back tears. "But you did make a choice. I asked you to come with me . . . just about begged you to . . ."

"Stop, OK?" Lina pushed herself up to her feet. "Just stop."

"It's true."

"It's a lie." She turned and headed for the door.

"Your nightmares . . . I think they're about the night I left." Lina stopped, but didn't turn around. "There was a storm . . . the wildest lightning . . . You were crying, and I came into your room."

"Where was Father?"

"The same place he probably is right now."

"The embassy."

"The embassy. I'd agreed to leave before he got home. He didn't want there to be a scene, and I basically agreed with him. I think for different reasons though." She pulled a chair over and sat in front of Lina. "A friend of mine had come to pick us up, we had a ten o'clock flight, I'd . . ."

"We?" Lina glared at her.

"You and me. I'd packed all of your things, and I came into your room to get you. You were hiding . . . curled into the littlest ball beneath your sheets . . . I thought you were afraid of the storm, so I told you a story about the 'rainmakers' and how they bring new life to the earth . . ."

185

An image flashed through Lina's mind, and she struggled to grasp, to hold it. "You were standing next to my bed . . . the lightning was flashing through the window behind you . . . you seemed so tall, almost like . . ."

"A tower?" Lina remained silent. Her mother shifted uncomfortably, then stood and walked to the window. "Nothing I said seemed to calm you down. You were so terrified, but I didn't understand. And then you looked up at me with those huge dark eyes and said 'Mommy I don't want to go. Don't make me go.' " She wiped the back of her hand up her cheek, catching a tear.

"I couldn't leave Father . . ."

"I understand. Part of me knew from the start I'd have to leave you behind. That's why I stayed for so long . . . but I couldn't do it anymore."

"Why?" Lina came up behind her. "Why couldn't you just stay?"

"Lina . . ." She turned, and Lina forced herself to meet her gaze. "I was suffocating there. I tried to explain that to you, but you were just too young."

"Not too young for you to walk out on, though."

"Your father gave me an ultimatum. I hated him for a long time for that . . . but in retrospect, he was right. None of us were happy. He needed a different type of woman on his arm. I just didn't fit in where he was going. I tried to change, but it wasn't working. We had a huge blowout after an embassy function one night. I wasn't dressed right, I made him look bad . . ." She half-smiled. "And then there was the tattoo."

"My tattoo?"

She nodded. "You wanted it so badly. You saw mine . . . I think you said you wanted to be twins." Her smile broadened. "It's a Gypsy symbol, you know. The triangle's the three mystic ladies, the goddesses of fate, who —"

"Come to the bed of every newborn child. Past, Present and Future." Lina averted her eyes and stared out at the flashing sign. "And the moon is the mother . . ."

"I've visited your dreams in many forms. I'm only sorry they've frightened you. As for the tattoo, I just couldn't say no to you. Your father always hated that about me — 'spare the rod' and all. So I took you to a friend of mine while he was away. I thought if it was just a little one, somewhere no one would ever see it . . ." She smiled. "You were so excited about it, you ran right up and showed it to him before he even got in the door. 'I'm a Gypsy,' you yelled. 'I'm a Gypsy' . . ." She shook her head. "You were his little girl. Always."

"That's why you left me?"

"Lina . . . leaving you was like drinking poison. It's never left me, it's still in my system. I don't expect you to understand this, but I was thirsting in so many ways that I drank what I knew would kill me just to save my life."

Lina wished she didn't understand what she was hearing. She wanted to stay mad. The only thing that had gotten her this far was the charge of her anger. But she knew she was hearing the truth. Bits and pieces she could remember, and years of experience with her father told her the rest. "I'd like to say I forgive you, but it wouldn't be true. Not yet."

"I understand. I'm grateful just to have you here."

"I planned this out for a long time."

"I guess." She smiled. "It's not like you were just passing through the neighborhood."

"No. Not like that at all."

"How did you find me?"

"The letter you sent asking Father for money."

"That was three years ago. And it went to the embassy. How'd you get your hands on it?"

"A strange twist of fate."

"You do believe in fate . . ."

"That's not what I meant." Lina tugged at a dangling curl and realized her mother was doing the same. "An attaché handed me the letter to give to him. He didn't know any better. I recognized the writing."

"You did?"

"From a card you gave me. I've always kept it with me, I don't know why."

"Amelia Earhart . . ."

Lina nodded. "The handwriting was the same. First I just noticed that it looked like mine. I ducked into a bathroom, read it . . . I was totally shocked. I didn't know he was in contact with you."

"We weren't. That was the agreement. We both thought it'd be better. At least he did." She turned to the window. "But I didn't want to screw up your life anymore either, so I promised I'd disappear."

"But you wrote."

"That was the first and last time. I was really

struggling, and I thought if I could just open up a little place of my own . . ."

"This place?"

She nodded. "He paid for it. I think he felt responsible for me in some odd way, and he was never a man to shirk responsibility. I'm paying him back though — it's almost really mine."

Lina joined her by the window. "I was so excited to know you were here, and *so* angry at the same time."

"Is that why you waited three years?"

"Oh, no. I was on it right away, but all I had to go on was a P.O. box number. You didn't make it easy. No car, no property, not registered to vote . . . I almost didn't find you."

"Where'd you look?"

"I did a little investigative work on my computer. I knew you were in the Seattle area, and using your maiden name. I checked every few weeks for almost a year waiting for *this* place to show up on some record somewhere, and finally it did."

"That's my girl." She smiled with all the pride of a mother.

"While I was searching for you, I happened upon some information about the university. I figured I should apply, just in case I found you. I knew I'd have to tell Father something."

"He *must've* been suspicious."

"I don't think so. I applied to eight different schools to cover my tracks. I just said I wanted to study in the States. All eight schools accepted me. I picked here."

"How long have you been here?"

"Almost a year. I came by this place the day after

I got into town, loitered around outside for awhile. It was so strange to see you."

"You've passed by a lot since then. Why'd you finally venture in?"

"The nightmares maybe. I don't know. I guess I finally knew they had something to do with you. And I'm leaving for home in two weeks. I knew I had to accomplish what I came here to do. And then Alex laid into me about family..."

"Alex?" She raised an eyebrow. "The woman who came for the reading."

"I work for her family."

"I saw you once with her and the boy."

"Sean."

"She pulled all four of the 'Daughter' cards... 'Past', 'Present', 'Future' and 'Self. It totally threw me. I knew it meant something, it was just too strange to believe — which drove me even crazier because I *live* by intuition." She reached sideways and touched Lina's shoulder. "But that night when I found you out front, when I touched you... I knew."

"Well..." Lina fixed her hair as a way to get the hand off her shoulder. "Now that we both know what we need to know, I'll be going."

"It's late. Why don't you stay? There's fresh sheets on the bed in the back room. I'll sleep on the couch."

"I have to work in the morning."

"I'll wake you first thing."

"No, really. I can't."

"I'll grind some Starbucks and send you flying at first light. And I make a mean French toast, with strawberries."

Lina remembered French toast with strawberries.

But she was determined not to bend, not to fold. "I can't."

"Lina . . ." She moved in front of her. "I don't know when I'll get to see you again. If you have any sense of what that means to me . . . as a mother . . . please stay the night." She reached and touched Lina's hair. "Please."

Lina stared at her mother, whose figure was dark and outlined by the red glow of "Futures Told" neon. Her body blocked most of the letters, and when Lina allowed her mind to drift, just a little, she realized that what she could actually read of the sign said only "F . . . old." The sign said "Fold." The sign . . . said fold.

17

The sky was ribboned with orange and pink, and Lina sped up the hill at full attention, hands off the handle bars, swaying her body to guide and keep balance. The morning seemed alive, or maybe it was just the Starbucks coffee pulsing through her blood.

"Go with the breath of the wind," her mother had said as they'd hugged good-bye. It had actually felt like a poetic moment, until her mother had been compelled to add a final word. "And don't trick yourself about that woman. Alex. She's in love with you."

"Don't play psychic with me," Lina had shot back, mostly to distract from her embarrassment.

"Oh, it's way worse than that." Her mom shook her head. "I think I'm playing mom."

They'd had their first good laugh about that, and Lina felt a heavy weight drop away. And as she now pedaled up the driveway, she actually felt delight upon finding Alex in her usual spot by the pool. "Hey." She pedaled up beside her and leaned against the lounge chair. "I'd like to speak with you."

Alex pulled her Ray-Bans down over her eyes. "I'm busy."

"Come on, don't do that with me. Please."

"*Don't do that with you*? Are you fucking kidding me? You drag your wandering ass in here from being out all night and you think you have a leg to stand on with me?" Lina couldn't help but smile. "What's so goddamn funny?" Alex's voice cracked.

"I was with my mother."

"You're right. That's pretty damn funny." She grabbed a smoke and slid her lighter out of her bikini bottom. "Is this what you were trying to tell me last night? That you've got someone else on the side?"

Lina slid down off her bike and laid it on the patio. "Listen. It *is* what I wanted to talk with you about. That's the truth."

"A little too little, a little too late." Alex lit her smoke.

"I came here, to Seattle, to track down my mother. I haven't seen her in years."

"Your mother's dead. Either that or you're a liar, in which case nothing you say holds any weight with me."

"Alex . . . I did lie. But I've always lied about it, so it felt like the truth."

"That's a total cop-out."

"That's what lying is, right? A total cop-out. I was ashamed of not telling you, but I guess I was more ashamed to tell you."

"Ashamed of what?"

"That psychic you went to . . . that's her."

"That's your mom?" Alex raised her glasses. "You're bull-shitting me." Lina locked her eyes on the pool and shook her head. Alex pulled herself up in her chair. "That's awesome . . . How come you got her and I got Claire?"

" 'The grass is always greener' comes to mind."

"So why the big secret? You had to know I'd think it was cool."

"*I* didn't think it was cool. It didn't feel cool to never see her, to have all these fantasies and then find out she's a fortune teller."

"She's a Gypsy. It's in her blood. It's in yours too, like a fire. I can feel it when we make love." Alex ran her hand up Lina's thigh. "Which, by the way, I've been missing."

Lina burned under Alex's touch. "I feel at peace about it now. I did what I needed to do."

"So . . ." Alex smiled and slid a finger along the edge of Lina's panties. "I guess you'll be staying."

Lina felt her heart sink. "I . . . I can't stay, Alex. I thought you understood. Especially now."

Alex withdrew her hand. "Especially now what?"

"My mother walked out on our family. I had to make peace with that. But I certainly won't turn around after all that and do the same thing."

"But that's exactly what you're doing. Don't you get it?"

Lina stood. "I do love —"

"Don't you dare." Lina felt Alex's stare shoot right through her. "Don't . . . you . . . dare!"

Lina lifted her bike. "I'm sorry you feel that way." She gripped it tightly and steered back to the cabana. There was no other way.

Her dreams were not tame over the days and nights that followed, but they were clear and simple. There was anxiety about exams, which were thankfully over — and there were dress rehearsals for her own departure . . . and for Alex's, which was underway that very moment.

"You wouldn't leave without saying good-bye, would you?" Lina pushed Alex's door open and leaned in.

Alex stuffed several shirts in a bag. "Talk to any of my exes."

Lina entered tentatively. "I have to go back. I promised my father I would."

"Yeah, well, a promise is a promise."

"I'm leaving next Friday, and I've told my father that if he can take a holiday, I'd like to spend a month in France with him. He has a lot of family there and . . ."

"Oh, a family reunion. How nice."

"I think it would be good for him. He . . . *we* haven't seen any of them since we moved to Greece."

Alex stopped packing and looked at Lina. "I'm

sorry. I know I'm supposed to be grown up about this, but I'm feeling about twelve right now. So let's just let it go, OK?"

Lina sat on the edge of the bed and looked around the room. "You know, this was my room before you came home."

Alex zipped her bag. "Well you can have it again, as of now."

"That's my intention."

Alex slung her bag over her shoulder and headed out the door. Sean rushed down the hall to meet her. "I could carry your bag."

"Thanks, sweetie." Alex stooped and kissed him on the forehead. "But I've got it."

Lina stepped into the hall, and Sean tugged on Alex's shirt. "How many days till Lina gets back here? More than you, or the same many?"

Alex glared at Lina. "You need to talk to her about that."

Sean turned to Lina. "How many days till you get back here? More than her, or the same many?"

"What did I tell you, buddy?"

Sean put a finger to his lips. "You're gonna make your dad go visit your grandma . . . and some other people . . . and then stay here with me again like before . . . and get your 'p' . . . 'p' . . ."

"Ph.D. You're a good listener." She rubbed his head.

Alex poked Lina in the side. "You little shit."

"She said 'shit'!" Sean tugged Lina's shirt.

Lina lifted Alex's bag and handed it to Sean. "Be a good boy and carry this out to the car," she imitated Claire's voice. "We'll talk more later."

Alex watched in shock as Sean took off with the bag. "Why didn't you tell me?"

"I wanted to straighten out the arrangements first. Nathan said I can continue living here, which I will for awhile but only until I find a place I can afford."

"Any four walls and a bed will do. On second thought, the bed's superfluous — and I do know what that means."

"Alex? Darling?" Claire's voice called from the foyer. Alex pushed Lina backwards into the guest bathroom and locked the door behind them. "Darling, where are you?" Claire's voice was getting closer.

"Mon Dieu . . ."

Alex put her hand over Lina's mouth. "I'm on the can, Mom. I'll meet you out by the car." Only after Claire's heels had clicked off down the hall did Alex remove her hand and replace it with her lips. "Today's our anniversary, you know," she whispered. "Three weeks and four days." She lifted Lina and planted her on the marble sink.

Lina realized she'd never had an anniversary before. "It's a start."

"A drop in the bucket, I hope."

Lina held Alex's face against hers. *"Je t'aime."*

"I warned you about speaking French," Alex whispered, running her hands up Lina's thighs.

"Mon amour . . ." Lina took Alex by the wrists and mischievously stretched her arms behind her back.

"You're torturing me."

"Do you like it?"

"Too early to tell." She smiled.

Lina pulled Alex between her legs. *"Jaimevais faire l'amour avec toi."* She kissed her way down Alex's neck. *"Ici . . ."* She pulled the snaps of her jeans open. *"Maitenain . . ."*

"Is that the same as 'fuck me'?"

"Close enough."

Alex bent her head back and closed her eyes. *"Oui . . ."*

"So, will we be seeing you for Christmas, darling?" Claire pulled Alex into a hug while Nathan loaded her bags into the trunk.

"That you will." Alex squeezed Claire and lifted her off the ground.

"Oh my . . ." Claire tittered.

"And Thanksgiving." Alex playfully dropped her.

"And Easter?" Sean hugged Alex around the knees.

"And Easter." She twisted her fingers through his curls.

"And Ground Hog's Day." Nathan laughed and reached for Alex, sandwiching Sean.

"Don't forget Lincoln's Birthday." She chuckled.

"And George Washington's Birthday," Sean's words were muffled.

"And Valentines Day, perhaps?" Nathan winked at Lina over Alex's shoulder.

Lina winked back without a moment's worry about propriety. "And Bastille Day."

"In the meantime . . ." Alex walked over and

pulled Lina into a hug. "I'd like to schedule a few appointments with Zack." She kissed Lina quickly on the lips and hopped into her car. She flipped down the convertible roof and revved the engine. "Bye, you guys." She waved as she backed down the driveway.

As the family made their way back into the house, they heard the screech of tires pulling off down the street. Lina scanned the faces around her for reaction.

"That's my girl." Claire smiled, signaling permission for the group to break into laughter. "PLG sandwiches anyone? Mom's cooking." She clicked down the hall toward the kitchen."

The pool lights reflected a splash of tiny stars onto the ceiling as Lina settled onto Alex's bed and lit a candle. She dialed online, and watched the hourglass flash as she uploaded her disk. Little by little, the GIF painted itself across the screen. A picture of herself that she'd had scanned just that day, after gulping down the compulsory PLG sandwiches.

It felt strange to be looking at her own image — seeing herself, seeing her mother, seeing a new person she didn't yet recognize but looked forward to knowing better. A person that Alex had beckoned, breathed life into, set free and captured at the same time.

She scrolled through the fonts in search of the one that best matched her mood. She settled on

"Bold Greek," and typed a caption at the bottom of her picture.

MON AMOUR, JE T'ENBRASSE ...

She kissed two fingers, touched them to the screen, and hit SEND — then played eleven hands of blackjack before diving into technicolor dreams.

A few of the publications of
THE NAIAD PRESS, INC.
P.O. Box 10543 • Tallahassee, Florida 32302
Phone (904) 539-5965
Toll-Free Order Number: 1-800-533-1973
Mail orders welcome. Please include 15% postage.
Write or call for our free catalog which also features an
incredible selection of lesbian videos.

BABY, IT'S COLD by Jaye Maiman. 256 pp. 5th Robin Miller
Mystery.   ISBN 1-56280-141-4 $19.95

WILD THINGS by Karin Kallmaker. 240 pp. By the undisputed
mistress of lesbian romance.   ISBN 1-56280-139-2   10.95

THE GIRL NEXT DOOR by Mindy Kaplan. 208 pp. Just what
you'd expect.   ISBN 1-56280-140-6   10.95

NOW AND THEN by Penny Hayes. 240 pp. Romance on the
westward journey.   ISBN 1-56280-121-X   10.95

HEART ON FIRE by Diana Simmonds. 176 pp. The romantic and
erotic rival of *Curious Wine*.   ISBN 1-56280-152-X   10.95

DEATH AT LAVENDER BAY by Lauren Wright Douglas. 208 pp.
1st Allison O'Neil Mystery.   ISBN 1-56280-085-X   10.95

YES I SAID YES I WILL by Judith McDaniel. 272 pp. Hot
romance by famous author.   ISBN 1-56280-138-4   10.95

FORBIDDEN FIRES by Margaret C. Anderson. Edited by Mathilda
Hills. 176 pp. Famous author's "unpublished" Lesbian romance.
                                            ISBN 1-56280-123-6   21.95

SIDE TRACKS by Teresa Stores. 160 pp. Gender-bending
Lesbians on the road.   ISBN 1-56280-122-8   10.95

HOODED MURDER by Annette Van Dyke. 176 pp. 1st Jessie
Batelle Mystery.   ISBN 1-56280-134-1   10.95

WILDWOOD FLOWERS by Julia Watts. 208 pp. Hilarious and
heart-warming tale of true love.   ISBN 1-56280-127-9   10.95

NEVER SAY NEVER by Linda Hill. 224 pp. Rule #1: Never get involved
with . . .   ISBN 1-56280-126-0   10.95

THE SEARCH by Melanie McAllester. 240 pp. Exciting top cop
Tenny Mendoza case.   ISBN 1-56280-150-3   10.95

THE WISH LIST by Saxon Bennett. 192 pp. Romance through
the years.   ISBN 1-56280-125-2   10.95

FIRST IMPRESSIONS by Kate Calloway. 208 pp. P.I. Cassidy
James' first case.   ISBN 1-56280-133-3   10.95

OUT OF THE NIGHT by Kris Bruyer. 192 pp. Spine-tingling
thriller.   ISBN 1-56280-120-1   10.95

NORTHERN BLUE by Tracey Richardson. 224 pp. Police recruits
Miki & Miranda — passion in the line of fire. ISBN 1-56280-118-X 10.95

LOVE'S HARVEST by Peggy J. Herring. 176 pp. by the author of
Once More With Feeling.   ISBN 1-56280-117-1   10.95

THE COLOR OF WINTER by Lisa Shapiro. 208 pp. Romantic
love beyond your wildest dreams.   ISBN 1-56280-116-3   10.95

FAMILY SECRETS by Laura DeHart Young. 208 pp. Enthralling
romance and suspense.   ISBN 1-56280-119-8   10.95

INLAND PASSAGE by Jane Rule. 288 pp. Tales exploring conven-
tional & unconventional relationships.   ISBN 0-930044-56-8   10.95

DOUBLE BLUFF by Claire McNab. 208 pp. 7th Detective Carol
Ashton Mystery.   ISBN 1-56280-096-5   10.95

BAR GIRLS by Lauran Hoffman. 176 pp. See the movie, read
the book!   ISBN 1-56280-115-5   10.95

THE FIRST TIME EVER edited by Barbara Grier & Christine
Cassidy. 272 pp. Love stories by Naiad Press authors.
                                            ISBN 1-56280-086-8   14.95

MISS PETTIBONE AND MISS McGRAW by Brenda Weathers.
208 pp. A charming ghostly love story.   ISBN 1-56280-151-1   10.95

CHANGES by Jackie Calhoun. 208 pp. Involved romance and
relationships.   ISBN 1-56280-083-3   10.95

FAIR PLAY by Rose Beecham. 256 pp. 3rd Amanda Valentine
Mystery.   ISBN 1-56280-081-7   10.95

PAXTON COURT by Diane Salvatore. 256 pp. Erotic and wickedly
funny contemporary tale about the business of learning to live
together.   ISBN 1-56280-109-0   21.95

PAYBACK by Celia Cohen. 176 pp. A gripping thriller of romance,
revenge and betrayal.   ISBN 1-56280-084-1   10.95

THE BEACH AFFAIR by Barbara Johnson. 224 pp. Sizzling
summer romance/mystery/intrigue.   ISBN 1-56280-090-6   10.95

GETTING THERE by Robbi Sommers. 192 pp. Nobody does it
like Robbi!   ISBN 1-56280-099-X   10.95

These are just a few of the many Naiad Press titles — we are the oldest and
largest lesbian/feminist publishing company in the world. We also offer an
enormous selection of lesbian video products. Please request a complete
catalog. We offer personal service; we encourage and welcome direct mail
orders from individuals who have limited access to bookstores carrying our
publications.